Understanding
Apples

For SARA:
Much Love and
many thanks.
A friend is a
friend, but an apple
is a rose...

JS Moore

JS MOORE

2007

Outskirts Press, Inc.
Denver, Colorado

Understanding Apples
All Rights Reserved

Outskirts Press
http://www.outskirtspress.com

ISBN-10: 1-59800-975-3
ISBN-13: 978-1-59800-975-0

Library of Congress Control Number: 2006934075

Outskirts Press and the "OP" logo are trademarks belonging to
Outskirts Press, Inc.

Printed in the United States of America

Upfront – let me just say that I am not – by any means – a writer. If anything, I would consider myself a storyteller. But I am surely not a writer – at least not a great one. In some circles storyteller means liar, but where I am from, it means just what the title is meant to imply. Not only are you invited to share in these stories, but there is a unique invitation waiting for you at the end of this book as well.

This collection of stories isn't meant to be read in one sitting. The people I've written about are real people. That said – some of the names had to be changed to protect the innocent as well as the guilty. Names that were not changed either had approval beforehand and after the stories were written by their loved ones – or are confirmed through public record.

Throughout this work (two and a half years of it!) you will see quotes by famous and not so famous individuals. Digest these words along with the stories that follow them.

You will see expressions we use here in the south in italics. When you see an expression like *his breath would knock a dog off a gut wagon* or *a bird in the hand is safer than one overhead*, please note that this is my respectful deference to a handful of fine individuals, characters from these stories, who use these phrases.

Suggested listening throughout the book is just what it says. It is merely a suggestion to tie in with whatever story the suggestion follows. It isn't the artist or recording company endorsing the story either.

Suggested listening: *Life's a Dance* by John Michael Montgomery

Preface

Like so many seedlings, saplings and trees in the woods, each one of us exhibits true uniqueness. Whether it is our external appearances, our size, shape, color or most importantly the internal characteristic that has sometimes been described as the fiber of our being. Yet, what brings us together as close friends and family are the similarities that we share with one another. Step back from the woods and see a compilation of green leaves and dark brownish grey bark, despite the possibility of hundreds of different species in that same tree line. The long range similarities are what allow us to come together despite the obvious differences in our actual character. This basic premise is what brought the author and me together as friends.

As a personal policy, I have avoided the acceptance of a personal definition. When asked how I might define myself, I try to see only the leaves and bark, and leave open the opportunity to become many things in the eyes of those who get to know me while I am alive. Unfortunately, to properly write the preface to this book, I am compelled to accept the fact that JS Moore met me as a busy, northern Yankee, business executive, and only after many conversations were he and I able to establish the similarities that existed between us. We met as an Oak and an Elm, a Maple and a Thorn Apple, but became simply trees in the woods over time.

I began traveling weekly to Johnson City, Tennessee in March 2005 from Buffalo, New York. During my stays in Tennessee, I talked with JS daily about the variety of subjects a Yankee out-of -towner, and Southern rooted man discuss. Football, the weather, local restaurants, problems at the airport, and of course, the previous weekend. Football discussions led to discussions about Marv Levy's[1] recently released book. As a result, our conversations lead to further discussions about the type of reading material we each prefer. Which lead to phrase that in my opinion 80% of American's say at one point or another, "If I were to write a book.....". Well I said it; further, I told Jason of an idea I had for a book. He responded, pleasantly surprised, with a discussion about a book he has been writing for some time. Our writings were/would be similar as we both were using trees as a basis for drawing parallels to human existence and life lessons. Jason and I discussed many things in the almost ten months I spent in Tennessee. But a parallel we enjoyed was routing those discussions to trees. If we discussed religion, one of us would note that trees have differing worship as well; some enjoy dry weather and sun, while others need excessive water. Yet the trees can coexist and respect the differing needs and worship. Rarely did we choose to discuss race, but if so, we could parallel that some trees do not cohabitate well with others because of their differing species; while other differing species thrived in the same environment.

In the end, we took that common interest in the tree and we used it to express our literary genius, although, I have to say that I do not believe literary genius actually exists. I think each of us may write, design and develop in whatever way we can, and strike only a similar chord with others through our words.

---

[1] Marv Levy was the coach of the Buffalo Bills football team during the four years the team appeared in the Super Bowl (and lost!!!). He had many quips and sayings that he compiled into a book about football and life's lessons.

It is not literary genius; it is being able to convey in text what others are feeling in their heart and mind. So when they read those words, they see the similarities and they are touched. To that end I cannot stress enough the need for anyone and everyone to read this book. As I noted above, JS and I were nothing alike. We used to laugh often at our dissimilarities. But what was most interesting when I began to read the pages of *Understanding Apples* is that I began to see myself in great detail. I like to see the romantic and dramatic side of things. I like to think that new places have such deep-rooted cultures. Coming from Buffalo, NY, and never having really traveled until my mid-twenties, I enjoy encountering and romanticizing the many cultural differences to be found across this vast country of ours. Then I read this book. When I was first in Tennessee, it struck me that people referred to their grandmother and grandfather "mamaw" and "papaw", and I easily romanticized it as a thread of the southern culture. When I would walk the streets, or go to the gym to work out, I would constantly relate anything different from the North as deep southern styles and traditions.

Now I am the great grandson of an Irish immigrant, a very typical lineage of Northeastern cities. The Irish came to working on the railroad and in the grain mills. And in my part of town, their sons and daughters became policemen and firemen, or worked at the local steel mill. And then their sons and daughters went to college, and that's where I am today; a college grad and great grandson of an Irish immigrant. Some years back I got a tattoo of my family crest. As I researched my genealogy, I uncovered the real details of being the great grandson of an Irish immigrant. I learned on my father's side that I was the grandson of an artist, who was in turn the son of a concert pianist. And I thought how wonderful it was to have those unique roots in America, and how they set me so far apart from people who grew up in the South (or other regions). Yet, as I read JS's book, I realized the many similarities *between JS and I. Despite all of his southern traditions that I created in my head, I was shocked to read that JS was adopted, and his "papaw" was through this paternal relationship. And further, that his true name was not Moore at all, but that was the name his "papaw" took to avoid trouble with the law. As I continued to read, I recognized more and more common threads, that my leaves and bark are no different from his. He loved his mother dearly, and his grandfather even more. I lost my father when he was 55, much too young to die. Too young for me to get to know him truly. But people now tell me how I remind them of my father, and I realize how much he must have taught me. What becomes more interesting is that since his death I have learned that my grandfather (his dad) was a drunk, but still an artist as well. And he too died at an early age of poor health. I also learned that his father was an orphan after one of his parents, I don't know which one, committed suicide and the other parent left him and his sister for adoption. Perhaps some of what my father taught me at an early age came from his experiences in life.*

*And then I also thought back to JS's grandfather and the lessons to JS within the stories of this book; and how he had to change his name due to problems with the law, and how neither of our **grandfathers** were exactly "upstanding" citizens. I sat and contemplated how similar JS and I are, so strong and rich in our traditions, but in the end, so similar in our life's realities. In my mind, that is really what this book is about – the realities of life and the values and lessons we learn from them. It is about understanding where you come from, and learning about the values and lessons that your family has taught you. And those values and lessons are your realities, my friends, and I say that not in jest. After reading this book, I now pass many people each day and understand a little better how they may be very much like me. This book has helped me see things in a different light. It has helped me look at that person whom I might not consider otherwise. I now realize that* *how they were raised, and how their family impacted them, taught them their values over time. And I think how similar they might be to me if I knew their truth. I implore you as you read this book to step back and see the forest and not the individual trees. Read this book and understand that you are reading about the lessons that Jason has learned in his life based upon what he was taught, based upon what he saw in his family. If I were to meet Judd Moore and he were to tell me of his life, I must admit that due to my conservative Yankee ways, with strong belief in what is right and wrong, I might not hold in high regard the man who once murdered, fought and wound up in a ditch. But when I think back to my college years, I believe my friends found me in a ditch or two. Anyways, not only are JS and I alike in our reality, but perhaps I was more like Judd Moore than I would like to admit, and that scares me slightly. And possibly that is why I try to teach children in my family better straighter ways, strong lessons and good values. But beyond that, the book also showed me how similar we as humans are when you look at our lives as you look at the forest from afar. Green leaves and dark bark, understanding the different species, but seeing the similarity in ourselves. As you read this book, look for the similarities in your life, and tomorrow when you see others, understand how they are really very much like you. Understand that they had families that shaped their ways; they had lifestyles that taught them values. Learn about life, understand the apple. Know that each person you see has leaves, trunks, and roots; making them who they are, just like you. Thank you JS for allowing me to write the preface. More importantly, thank you for the opportunity to read Understanding Apples and take from it something special.*

-Michael J. Burns

Table of Contents

As different as two great trees which grow side by side, Judd Moore and his only son stood tall in my eyes, sharing and sheltering the world of my youth, yet possessing their own unique qualities. My father, Roger, is like the solid American elm, strong of character, enduring and possessing wisdom beyond his years. Papaw Judd, my grandfather, was the towering American chestnut, deeply rooted in the land, independent and the last of his kind.

Intro

Apples, throughout history, have come to symbolize choices - from the story of Genesis with Adam and Eve sampling the fruit of the Tree of Knowledge and defying God to the fairy tale of Snow White, bound by the laws of hospitality, accepting a poisoned apple from the haggard old crone. In one well-known Greek myth, Hercules achieves immortality by eating a sacred apple. Wasn't Sir Isaac Newton given a choice when hit on the head by that falling fruit? And what about William Tell's only son standing erect with an apple upon his head for target practice? No matter how good a shot my father might be with a bow and arrow, I think I would have high-tailed it home that go round. Is life just a never ending series of choices?

Choices that we inevitably pay for in one way or another.

Understanding Apples. Our lives are all interwoven like the ornate branches of a solitary amalgamated apple tree. A green red or yellow fruit represents each one of us. Some of us are sweet and some of us are sour. Some are ripe, and some downright rotten. There are the juicy varieties as well as the bitter fruits upon this tree. But within each of us there lays a choice: a bright and shining star that is a living foundation of the fiber that generates who we are. Five seeds, if you will, that can be connected to form an endless and blazing continuum. There are five different virtues that must be offered as each seed. Every individual person is unique; therefore, no assembly of people will possess exactly the same qualities.

Originally, I began *Understanding Apples* to serve as a living history and record of one man: Judd Moore. But, delving deeper into the pages of his life, I soon found that his story could not be told in true reflection or all honesty without including those other people I have often cared for, sometimes disliked, but come to appreciate and respect - mostly for taking the time shape me into who I am today. Who am I? Well, who are you? We ask ourselves this very question pretty much our whole lives.

Like many folks in the world, my family history is crawling with stories that are often repeated, widely known, yet completely untrue. However, my opinion is that myths have at least a grain of truth to them, and in many cases, the truth is more interesting than the myth. I have always enjoyed myths, the true ones and the not-so-true ones. With *Understanding Apples*, I probably will not dispel any of these beliefs from the hearts and minds of people who knew my relations. I just think sometimes people need to be reminded that stories are interesting enough without having to make them up.

Anyone that knows the city of Kingsport in Tennessee, the Model City, our "Little Apple", knows about *Church Circle* and the area adjacent to it: *Five Points*, quite a seedy area to this very day. For a moment let's examine this fine town – the way it is now and the way it used to be.

It used to be that Kingsport, Tennessee wasn't King's Port at all. It was Christianville prior to King's Port, but well before that the area was part of a Cherokee nation – so vast – and so rich in agriculture and history, oral history, the area was actually a sacred ground to the Native Americans. What is called Long Island here in Kingsport, Tennessee was once a hallowed stretch – a four and a half mile island that was nestled between the Holston River and the Sluice, revered by the tribesman for its energy and spiritual presence. Before 1776 and the Battle of Long Island Flats it was said that no man could be killed on Long Island. But in 1777 the chiefs of all seven clans gathered and signed a treaty with the white man, giving up not only hundreds of thousands of their acreage, but millions – including the sacred ground known as Long Island. Because the chieftains' decision was not unanimous among the elders or their sons – a powerful curse was placed upon the hallowed ground: No man would ever find peace there.

A mere window of events is shared within the pages of this book that offer only a glimpse of what life was like thereafter.

Thanks for reading,

JS Moore

Suggested Listening: *Choices* by George Jones

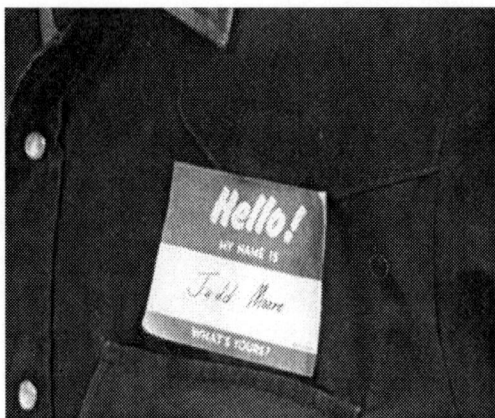

For my Dad, Roger Moore.

UNDERSTANDING

Halved

If you want to make an apple pie from scratch, you must first create the universe.

-Carl Sagan

T ake an apple – any apple - and hold it in your hand with the stem on top. Pretend, if you will, that this savory fruit is the earth. Take a knife and cut the globe across its equator – the center. Open up the halved fruit and examine its insides. How many seeds are present? Count them. Five seeds, right? Those seeds nestled with the apple's core form a star. Do you see the star? Now take a bite of this forbidden fruit.

The five pointed star was what an Arthurian knight had blazoned upon his shield. Each point to this star represents one of the five core values or *virtues* of chivalry: Honor, Courage, Generosity, Forgiveness, and Loyalty. Five Points. I may upset the *Powers That Be* for sharing this, but in Masonic practices, ancient and contemporary, there are *five* perfect *points* of Entrance. Those points have evolved through the years as well.

There were thirteen virtues that Benjamin Franklin, a Mason himself, felt were necessary to try to follow to have a good and moral character:

Temperance: Eat not to dullness; drink not to elevation

Order: Let all your things have their places; let each part of your business have its time.

Silence: Speak not but what may benefit others or yourself; avoid trifling conversation

Resolution: Resolve to perform what you ought; perform without fail what you resolve.

Frugality: Make no expense but to do good to others or yourself; i.e., waste nothing.

Industry: Lose no time; be always employed in something useful; cut off all unnecessary actions.

Sincerity: Use no hurtful deceit; think innocently and justly, and, if you speak, speak accordingly.

Justice: Wrong none by doing injuries, or omitting the benefits that are your duty.

Moderation: Avoid extremes; forbear resenting injuries so much as you think they deserve.

Cleanliness: Tolerate no uncleanliness in body, cloths, or habitation.

Tranquility: Be not disturbed at trifles, or at accidents common or unavoidable.

Chastity: Rarely use venery but for health or offspring, never to dullness, weakness, or the injury of your own or another's peace or reputation.

Humility: Imitate Jesus and Socrates.

It is important to understand that no one is perfect. Ben Franklin himself was known to overindulge in many things from wine-drinking and food to basking in the company of female companionship a bit more than most. He also said the only things he liked were "illegal, immoral, or fattening." But at least his intentions were purely positive. I guess that is the trick really, knowing right from wrong and at least trying to deter our human nature whenever possible.

At least for beginners, I like the idea of five core virtues better than Franklin's thirteen. Someone who can visualize their strengths as well as their weaknesses is what I call "the Halved." Someone who hasn't got a clue why they are special or what makes them unique *have their cart before their horse* in my opinion and are "the Halved-Nots." It is important to examine ourselves. God knows everyone else does.

From any journey - whether geographic or imaginative, the most important keepsake is the reminder that people's lives are fortified by family and friends; by our ability to create our lives like preparing an apple pie from scratch. There is and should always be a great and cherished appreciation for life itself and the priceless importance of our connections to one another.

Suggested Listening: *Johnny Appleseed* by Gene Autry

Seeds

All work and no play makes John a dull boy.
                              -Poor Richard's Almanack

There was once upon a time a little boy who was tired of all his toys and tired of all his play.

"What shall I do?" he asked his mother. And his mother, who always knew beautiful things for little boys to do, said, "You shall go on a journey and find a little red house with no doors and no windows and a star inside."

This really made the little boy wonder. Usually his mother had good ideas, but he thought that this one was very strange.

"Which way shall I go?" he asked his mother. "I don't know where to find a little red house with no doors and no windows."

"Go down the lane past the farmer's house and over the hill," said his mother, "and then hurry back as soon as you can and tell me all about your journey."

So the little boy put on his cap and his jacket and started out. He had not gone very far down the lane when he came to a merry little girl dancing in the sunshine. Her cheeks were like pink blossom petals and she was singing like a robin.

"Do you know where I shall find a little red house with no doors and no windows and a star in inside?" asked the little boy.The little girl laughed, "Ask my father, the farmer,she said. "Perhaps he knows."

So the little boy went on until he came to the great brown barn were the farmer kept a barrel of fat potatoes and baskets of yellow squashes and golden pumpkins. The farmer himself stood in the doorway looking out over the green pastures and yellow grain fields.

"Do you know where I shall find a little red house with no doors and no windows and a star inside?" asked the little boy of the farmer.

The farmer laughed, "I lived a great many years and I never saw one," he chuckled, "but ask Granny who lives at the foot of the hill. She knows how to make molasses, taffy and popcorn balls, and red mittens! Perhaps she can direct you."

So the little boy went on farther still, until he came to the Granny, sitting in her pretty garden of herbs and marigolds. She was wrinkled as a walnut and as smiling as the sunshine. "Please, Dear Granny," said the little boy, "where shall I find a little red house with no doors and no windows and a star inside?"

Granny was knitting a red mitten, and when she heard the little boy's question, she laughed so cheerily that the wool ball rolled off her lap and down the little pebbly path.

"I should like to find that little house myself," she chuckled. "I would be warm when the frosty night comes and the starlight would be prettier than a candle. Ask the wind that blows about so much and listens at all the chimneys. Perhaps the wind can direct you."

So the little boy took off his cap and tipped it politely to the Granny and went on up the hill rather sadly. He wondered if his mother, who usually knew almost everything, had perhaps made a mistake.

The wind was coming down the hill as the little boy climbed up. As they met, the wind turned about and went along, singing beside the little boy. It whistled in his ear, pushed him and dropped a pretty leaf into his hand.

"I wonder," thought the little boy, after they had gone along together for a while, "if the wind could help me find a little red house with no doors and no windows and a star inside."

The wind cannot speak in our words, but it went singing ahead of the little boy until it came to an orchard. There it climbed up in the apple tree and shook the branches. When the little boy climbed up, there at his feet lay a great rosy apple.

The little boy picked the apple. It was as much as his two hands could hold. It was red as the sun had been able to paint it, and the thick brown stem stood up as straight as a chimney, and it had no doors and no windows. Was there a star inside?

The little boy called to the wind, "Thank you," and the wind whistled back.

Then the little boy gave the apple to his mother. His mother took a knife and cut the apple through the center. Oh, how wonderful! There inside the apple, lay a star holding brown seeds.

"It is too wonderful to eat without looking at the star, isn't it?" the little boy said to his mother. "Yes indeed," answered his mother.

-Author Unknown

The story of Johnny Appleseed isn't only a legend but based upon a true story. Why was it necessary to plant apple trees in the United States? Fact: there were no apple trees in North America before the white man came to make a home here. The only variety that even comes close is the crabapple.

Suggested Listening: *Old Apple Tree* by Shirley Caesar

Stem

First, one must endure.

-Ernest Hemingway

Rowdy crowd – they were…any of them - back deep in a place called Rough Holler where folks got rougher and tougher the farther back they lived toward the mountain. The Moore family lived in the very last little clapboard house on the left on that dead end dirt road.

Judd Moore once said about Luck: the one time I pitched a horseshoe over my left shoulder it hit my Daddy in the back of the head. He chased me all over the farm, through the barn, and around the house with a single-tree. I had to hide up on Holston Mountain from him, scrounge the hills for poke salad, and one time share a meal with a railroad hobo for those few days while my Daddy cooled off.

In 1932, at fourteen years of age, with only the denim overalls he owned and a worn out pocketknife, Judd Moore set out from his home in Hickory Tree, Tennessee to wherever his bare-feet might take him. With a bracing autumn wind and orange hue at his back he headed southwest - away from Holston Mountain and the farm he had worked on throughout his childhood. There were no goodbyes to or from Martin Moore, his ill-natured father, whom lay unconscious on the hardwood floor in the front room. By the time the cock crowed loud to announce the sun's arrival Judd was three miles away from the farm and was already helping his self to a wild bramble breakfast picked from the dirt roadside.

The lashes he had received from Martin the night before striped his back and legs while the sting of those marks numbed the boy's mind with one goal – to get away while his legs would still function. He had fought back this time and grabbed the black snake whip from his father's grasp. He had punched the drunken man in the face with a force that would have brought down a bull. Then he tackled his father around the waist, bringing them both down onto the floor. Twice his father's head struck the hard floor, guided by the hands of an angry son who was tired of the abuse. Mrs. Moore, Judd's mother, had led the other children into the back room – perhaps knowing there would finally be such a reckoning. Winded by adrenaline and his actions, the youth tried to rise from his father's motionless heap but instead found himself too weak with even his greatest effort. He felt the patches of liquid on his own back begin to trickle out of the lacerations from the whip, the whip he found still clutched in his own left hand.

As the door to the back room creaked open and he saw his younger brother Jay's curious head peek into the front room, Judd felt his strength restored and slowly stood. "You finally got him. You finally did it," his brother had whispered. Speechless, Judd stared at his own shadow on the wall from the firelight of the hearth. His monstrous outline still held his father's black snake whip like a lion tamer. He had just accomplished what even his older brother Duke never did. He had whipped the man who had many times beaten his mother, brothers and sisters close to the point of death. His brother cautiously stepped into the room, maintaining eye contact with Judd. Then he looked to the hardwood floor in shock. And with an expression of hatred the younger boy kicked the unconscious man in the ribcage for good measure, managing a smile of relief that the drunk did not stir. Jay's wide eyes again met Judd's. Their mother entering the room interrupted the silence.

"I reckon' it's about time this happened, boys," she stated matter-of-factly, "Judd, it's time you left this God forsaken place. Just in case - you'd best not be here when he wakes. No regret, son. You did what we all needed you to."

His mother knelt down and reached into her husband's pant pockets, producing a pocketknife – which she handed to Judd. He put the piece away in the front pouch of his bib overalls then shook hands with his younger brother, Jay. His mother took up a poker and was tending the hearth's fire as her two sons left into the back room where the rest of the children waited in hushed whispers by candlelight. Huddled closely around the smaller boys, Sherman and Denny, Judd's sisters thanked their older brother Judd with just their eye contact as he headed toward the back door with Jay close behind.

Perhaps the expression *absence makes the heart grow fonder* is true because the result of Judd's reckoning with his father changed Martin Moore for good. He would miss his son's strong back on the farm. He would miss his son's take charge attitude when the other children weren't pulling their weight with the workload. The Moore children feared their father, made fun of him behind his back, but they respected their elder brother Judd and would pay attention to their brother's instruction. Martin never raised a hand to his wife or kids again.

Miles away now from the old Moore home place in Hickory Tree, Judd soon began to appreciate the rising sun at his back and the daylight. He knew, though, that many dangers would lie ahead of him. He began to hum to himself and made up a song from a saying his sister Carrie had coined:

"Martin Horton
Horse fart and snortin'
Is that how yer garden grew
You'd been a drinkin'
Breath all a stinkin'
Like a pile of donkey poo...,"

He stopped singing when he heard a vehicle approaching from behind. It was his Uncle Bill Collins driving up slow on the dirt road, but Judd didn't know it. It could have been the authorities, so he took off running at a sprint away from the path. Hitting every puddle and hole in his approach, Bill stopped alongside where his nephew had leapt into the weeds. Bill shouted with the driver side window already down.

"Judd! C'mon. Let's go."

His uncles' round face was unshaven. His red hair was disheveled and needed attention. Judd rose from the thicket and looked cautiously back to the car.

"I ain't goin' back there!"

"I know boy. Need a lift where you're headed?"

"Dunno, sir. What do you think?" the boy answered.

"Hell yes you do," Bill offered, "Get in."

Judd was surprised in his luck and found relief until his back touched the passenger seat. His wounds were aching worse than ever and he tried to hide his pangs. His uncle already knew where to take Judd.

"I can take you as far as Kingsport to the foot of Bays Mountain where there is a logging outfit that may need some hard workers like yourself. Sound alright, Judd?"

"Sure, Bill. Sounds like my kinda place."

Bays Mountain and the Kingsport area at that time were undergoing a great bit of growth. George Eastman and other industrial businessmen had brought several businesses to the community and the Great Depression was something easily missed in the region known as the Tri-Cities because of the abundance of employment for any adult willing to work. But Judd was young, too young for them. When denied proper employment by anywhere he tried, he decided to continue on to whatever the highest point was he could see in the area, Chimney Top Mountain. It rose in the distance like a huge volcano but it was miles and miles of rough country away.

Suggested Listening: *Rain on the Scarecrow/Crumblin' Down/Your Life Is Now* by John Mellencamp, *Country Boy* by Johnny Cash

Gravity

Every object in a state of uniform motion tends to remain in that state of motion unless an external force is applied to it.
- Sir Isaac Newton

Old Man Taylor lived at the foot of Chimney Top Mountain. He was an ornery cuss, older than the dirt they'd dug up to bury his poor wife. He had her placed beneath a sprawling Cottonwood tree - for winter was her favorite season - and during the summer, when the giant tree shed its coat, it was if snow were falling to cover her unmarked grave.

"You'll step lightly around this hallow ground," he told the boy, pointing out an imagined perimeter around the site.

"Yes, sir," the boy agreed, without questioning his gaunt and humped-back elder.

"Ah hell son, ye don't have to call me 'sir' - call me Old Man, or sum-bitch. I could care less. But don't call me 'sir'."

The boy had never met someone who didn't mind being called old. And certainly not someone who would answer to Old Sum-bitch, which is what he called him whenever they were cutting up. The majority of the time Judd respectfully found himself calling him Mr. Taylor. The old man was the closest thing to a father he would ever know. They hit it off from the *gitgo* and the boy grew into a man under the old man's tutelage. He stood five feet nine inches now and his body was muscular like some statue from Greek mythology. There wasn't an ounce of fat on his chiseled frame. Working hard day in and day out would toughen any young man who labored constantly and without fail to earn his keep. Young Judd helped to run seventy five acres of farm land for Old Man Taylor a number of years. He also performed odd jobs like cutting the grass, shoveling manure from the stables and spreading it out in the gardens as fertilizer, and transporting spirits to whatever destination he was instructed. In exchange for his diligence, he received a roof over his head, two meals a day, and made some coin in the process. The value of a quarter or even a nickel was golden to the young Judd. And fresh water and food, the sustenance many folks often take for granted, was something he learned to treasure, too, like a breath of clean air or money in his pockets.

Gambling was a vice soon introduced to a then seventeen year old Judd Moore. After losing a good deal of money to an obnoxious stranger called Hatchet with questionable card playing techniques in the rafters of

Taylor's barn, Judd found himself in a situation he'd not been in since he stood up against his own father Martin. The provocation led to an old-time country brawl and the tussle was pretty even until Judd walloped Hatchet across the face with a three foot pig iron. Then, in a fit of uncontrolled rage, Judd fashioned a noose from a strand of hemp rope and placed it firmly around the man's throat. After tying the rope to a sturdy post, he kicked Hatchet over the side and hanged him. Pure emotion and anger peppered with a mix of strawberry wine and a long day of work had charged Judd with this merciless action. Hatchet reached up onto the rope and held on for dear life, gurgling and swearing he'd seek revenge.

Judd fled the property, knowing he would now be a wanted man. But he didn't know that Old Man Taylor had stirred with all the commotion and had actually cut Hatchet down before he could suffocate completely. Hatchet lived and so did a warrant for Judd Moore's arrest. Back then, though, records had a habit of disappearing. And Old Man Taylor, it is believed, bought off the authorities. Within several weeks Judd could rest easy that the law wasn't looking for him any longer. He settled in the area of Green Shed and found work with Old Man Taylor's nephew Frank Hall.

Suggested Listening: American Trilogy/I'll Remember You/Stand By Me by Elvis Presley

Switches

Too bad all the people who know how to run the country are busy driving cabs and cutting hair.

-George Burns

John Robert Cleek and his younger brothers Carl Thomas and Werner Eugene were from an area called Chestnut Ridge in Weber City, Virginia. They ran a Long Island cabstand in Kingsport, Tennessee for a good number of years during and after Prohibition. John and Carl were both business savvy individuals and both men understood an opportunity they could cash in on when it presented itself. Since Tennessee remained a "dry" state after Prohibition was dissolved in 1933 the men networked out of the city, making vital connections to local bootleggers as well as distanced suppliers as far as New York and Chicago. When someone called the cabstand stating they "needed picked up" it didn't mean they needed to go somewhere. The same goes if they called and said they "needed a lift" or "needed a ride". Those terms were all code for they needed something alcoholic to drink or some female companionship or some other prohibited goods. The cab company was a multi-purpose delivery service in every sense of the word. If someone needed to go somewhere they would usually give the location they were and where they were headed to.

Once the Cleek Bros. resourceful brother Harry was of a useful age they put him to work as well. These boys had literally came from nothing and built an empire in Kingsport - respectfully. Everyone knew the vast majority of politicians were corrupt in the Model City. And it was understood that most officers in law enforcement could be swayed by that corruption. But if the police could be swayed by the upper crust then they could be bought off by the bottom layer, too.

The Cleek Brothers operated under several aliases. To patrons they were "the Clicks" – spelled the way the name is pronounced here in the Tri-Cities with our slow and southern enunciating twang. Kind of like the word creek is pronounced her in the area: crick. Each brother had their own nickname as well. Buck, Zeke, Boot, Hack, and later on their little brother James Patten took on an even more colorful alias: "Bill".

The Click cabs and their other transportation vehicles were fast. They ran just as fast in reverse as they did forward. This was necessary to outrun the law, the revenuers, and the ABC (Alcohol Beverage Control) Men. The yellow and black Cadillac of Zeke and later Buck Click was many times given chase but never ever caught. Every auto or truck within the Click fleet had a modified chassis designed to look normal - even if they were loaded down with liquor. Rival bootleggers were often caught because the fuzz could tell they were hauling goods.

Before there was a NASCAR or professional racing as a sport there were numerous races in and around the Tri-Cities. Zeke Click, it has been told to me several times by numerous individuals, was undefeated on what is called "The Crooked Road" coming out of Newport – even besting drivers who would later make a name for themselves in the early beginnings of what is now NASCAR. Had Zeke Click been born a generation later – his name might have been synonymous with racing as well as bootlegging.

Suggested Listening: *Only Daddy That'll Walk the Line/ I'm a Ramblin' Man/Good Ole' Boys* by Waylon Jennings

Understanding Apples

"Even if I knew that tomorrow the world would go to pieces, I would still plant my apple tree."

--Martin Luther

J udd Moore liked to sit by the TV without it on, pocketknife in one hand, Red Delicious in the other, carefully splitting the apple down the middle while holding it whole in his hard and calloused hand. There was an art and simplicity to the ritual, both methodical and elegant. Another slice; now four pieces. Again; then doubled. Finally, with surgical precision, he would cut a semicircle around the core, extracting the seeds.

"Poison," he would say. Then he would ask, "How 'bout a sliver?"

"Sure."

It would be a rare thing for me to turn down the offer.

"Let me salt it just a smidgen."

It was his way. Seventeen years I watched him handle an apple with such care. He preferred the red ones, sweet and juicy. But sometimes those he held were golden; golden - like him. In my mind's eye, that color infuses all memories of this man I grew up watching, listening to, and emulating. Today I see his movements and manner described in my own. His thoughts, stories, and often times his curse words, find voice again in mine.

I never shared with him that salt, too, could be detrimental to someone's health; that his careful efforts to remove the seeds were in some ways cancelled out by that smidgen of salt. It never truly mattered. Biting into that sliver was always the same, as good as chocolate, but better for me.

Back then I used to analyze my actions and worry about the consequences. Like Adam and Eve in the Garden of Eden taking a bite of that forbidden fruit - was I defying God? I would note that such trees were all over my Grandparents property and my own parents as well. What knowledge would such partaking bring a young man like me? Or would it merely keep the Doctor away if I shared in a slice? Enjoying a Golden or Red Delicious about once or twice a week with my Papaw would not hurt my reputation as a rebellious youth too much anyway.

As a kid, I often climbed the towering trees in Papaw's yard - much like a monkey, but with less skill. Once, when I was nine years old, while hanging upside-down, my seventy-five pound body managed to break a large limb, sending me headfirst six feet or so to the soft grass without a single scratch. However, it was wound enough for the already aging apple tree, which had to be cut-down soon after. Papaw was nearly as prideful of those trees as he was his own children. He planted that particular tree in the Forties when they had first moved into the Springdale community. My dad was just a few years old when he watched my Papaw carefully place the seedling in the ground.

"This tree will grow up with you," he had explained.

My grandparents' yard was where my brother, my cousins, and I had many of our treasure quests, bank robberies, and gunslinger showdowns. I always wondered if my Dad had such great adventures when he was my age, with abundant trees to climb and endless games to play like Cowboys and Indians or Cops and Robbers or Tarzan the Ape Man. I began asking questions and those questions led to some terrific stories.

As a kid my Dad always spoke of his childhood with a glimmer in his eyes – talking about the legendary BB gun wars with the other neighborhood kids. The skirmishes involved real BB guns and real pain. You couldn't hide getting shot when they played.

Suggested Listening: *Song of the South/Born Country/Tennessee River/Mountain Music* by Alabama

Slices

I have always found that mercy bears richer fruits than strict justice.
- Abraham Lincoln

It was in the Fall of 1954. McCarthy had been condemned for misconduct. Racial segregation had been banned in public schools. And New York had won the World Series. My Dad was almost nine years old.

"Roger! Debbie," Opal hollered loudly from the porch steps, "Roger! Debbie! C'mon and wash-up for supper!"

Debbie heard her mother calling them.

"Ooh! Momma's going to tan your behind, Roger Moore. You just wait!"

She smiled as a little blood dripped down her left cheek. Suddenly, her face contorted into something more baby-like, her eyes welled up, and then tears began to fall like rain on a summer day when it is not wanted. Roger stood there still in shock with his hand shaking wildly and his pocketknife clutched loosely with the blade still open.

"Debbie," he mustered, "I am so sorry. It was an accident."

"Accident. Smackshident! You're gonna get it," she snapped with no longer a baby face, but more of an old musk turtle come out of it's shell. Face transforming again back to sobs she should have crawled back up the hill like a whiney toddler to the house. A light came on in Roger's head and like King Kong he scooped her up in his arms and held her close to his chest, walking swiftly toward their mother who awaited them on the porch. Debbie fought her brother at first, but then realized he was sincere in his apology. Accepting his courteous gesture, she was soon trying to gather her emotions to keep her father from finding it out.

"Deb honey you're bleeding!"

Opal noticed the cut before they were able to cross the driveway. The little girl's face was dried with dirt, blood, and salty tears: tears that burned her wind-chapped face. All of young Debbie's composure vanished as her mother took her from King Kong's mighty grasp. The gorilla looked away as silently to himself he asked God to help him whisk him away to the heavens atop the Empire State Building for a few days while things settled down at 1829 McKinney Street.

The cut was made while Roger was swinging his newly sharpened pocketknife in the high grass atop a hillside overlooking the garden. He had spent many days on his own among the fields and hills at the home place, blade of grass in his mouth like a cigarette. On this day Hoyt Bowen, his best friend, was out of town with his family, the Archers could not play, the Davenports all had Chicken Pox, and the Collins children had gone fishing with Charles Williams. Five-year old Debbie had been playing on the neighbors' new swing-set. She had sought her brother out when the Conkins had left to go to the grocery store. After finding him, she snuck through the high grass and quickly planned a prank to scare her daydreaming brother. But, with his arms in a whirlwind, he did not notice her leap up - no time to react - until it was too late.

"Stitches and switches," Opal remarked as she shook her head with disbelief. Roger knew all too much what this meant: a trip to the willow tree for just the right size switch. Their mother hurried, though, better her than her husband to handle this one.

"Be quick about it, Roger Judd. I'll be in the washroom fixing up your sister."

Debbie looked back over her mother's shoulder as she mouthed the words, "I'm sorry." "Me, too," Roger whispered.

"What was that? Get going, son. There'll be no backtalk," his mother commanded.

"Yes Ma'am," the boy shrugged, spying a small branch and another in case of breakage.

Within ten minutes, they heard the familiar rumble of their father's truck approaching. A shot rang loudly down the street, then another closer. The children knew there was no gun. The 1948 Dodge was as loud as gunfire on the frontline and as beat up as the wounded soldiers strung up in constantino wire. It was four feet high chicken wire in this case, framing the truck-bed like a cage just high enough to keep the critters in: mud turtles, cats, or whatever he saw fit.

Of the morning the old man would locate then catch a wild or stray cat, toss it into the truck-bed, and make off for work. No one really knew what he did with them, but good stews were served on the Island in those days. Ingredients were an Alvis family secret. If patrons were eating kitty cat, they didn't have a clue – and maybe they didn't care.

He growled under his breath before grabbing his lunchbox and swinging open the driver side door. Scanning over the backyard area silently, he knew something to be amiss. But what? The cigar in his mouth was removed, put out on an old rusted anvil just behind him, then placed on the dashboard of the truck for later. Shutting the door tight, he headed toward the house.

Although Roger's legs and bottom were very sore from the switching, he sat at the table patiently while trying not to cringe. Debbie's forehead was home to a small bandage - a knick to hide (yet, the scar is still there above her eye).

"Remember you two," Opal started, "I've already handled the punishment. He won't whip you twice, Roger."

This still seemed like quite a predicament for the two youngsters. Their father stepped in through the backdoor, placed his lunchbox on the counter, and moved passed the fridge to his seat at the head of the table.

"Wash those hands, Judd?" she asked.

He mumbled then nodded, "Before I left the shop."

They all took their seats. The children bowed their heads as their mother started the blessing. Their father sat upright, eyes open, watching them.

"Dear Lord," she began.

"Dear Lord," he interrupted, "whatever happened to your noggin, young lady?"

Debbie sat silent with her eyes tightly shut, her mouth almost gasping for air, then she opened one eye and glanced up at her father.

"It was an accident, Daddy," she managed, "I was gonna scare him."

"Let's have it," his father sternly said as he

extended his hand.

Roger stood, then reluctantly - dug into his jean pocket amidst the bolts, bands, ball cards, and a chicken feather, finding the cold brown pommel of his only pocketknife. Slowly he reached over and placed it into the solid right hand of his old man. Roger felt tears building up in under his eyes, but fought them back like Captain America battling the Nazi War Machine. Then his old man - in a single motion - lifted from the chair like a ghost, floated passed the fridge and his lunchbox, and out the backdoor. Opal nodded and Roger followed his father outside.

Judd shook with disappointment as he looked out from the driveway across the valley and into the woodland. A steady breeze blew as his eight-year old son made his way toward where he stood. A swirl of wind raised an orange leaf into the air, and then let it down. This was a most uncomfortable silence.

Across the field and into the forest but beyond it all, somewhere and somehow, the pocketknife sailed farther than any ancient warrior's spear could have flown. The eight-year old boy watched breathlessly as it disappeared from view.

"Roger," his father finally spoke, "you have got to watch out for your sister."

Those words sank into the boy's heart deeper than any blade.

Suggested Listening: I'm Just a Country Boy/Lord, I Hope This Day Is Good/Good Ole Boys Like Me/Till' The Rivers All Run Dry/I Believe In You by Don Williams

Tap Water

The problem with some people is that when they aren't drunk, they're sober.

-W.B. Yeats

Before tragedy slammed down onto her family - Goldie Dykes was a devout Christian. In the eyes of her congregation she was a fine example of a saintly woman and well respected by her peers. Bringing her children along with her, she attended church services any time the doors were open. Her husband Nip lay at home very ill. He couldn't work and so the once honest living that he brought in was dissolved to nothing but what little welfare and the kindness of others offered. Government cheese and peanut butter only went so far. Goldie prayed for her husband's health, but it only worsened. With bills piling up and a notice by the power company – Goldie prayed for God's Will, but she felt betrayed.

One day while she was away at the market her kids had accidentally trapped a good-sized muskrat down on the riverbank. They decided to skin the animal, cook it up in their momma's iron skillet, and have dinner ready whenever she got home.

"I ain't n'er had river skunk a'for," the youngest one said.

"It ain't no river skunk. Daddy calls it a 'swamp bunny,'" the oldest boy advised.

The middle boy first thought it to his self then said, "Momma and Daddy are gonna like hav'n meat with the taters."

When Nip Dykes, their father, had been healthy some time before, he had taught the older boys how to trap then dress an animal for its fur and sometimes its meat. Raccoon, rabbit, squirrel, fox, and muskrat hides all paid a fair amount. To them, their father was an expert furrier. But the boys weren't thinking about selling the animal's hide. They were only counting on providing some much needed nourishment for their bellies.

The younger boy carefully watched the messy work of his brothers, but soon found it unbearable. So he went inside and prepared the skillet and fired up the stove. Then he carefully set the table, trying hard not to make much noise because his father was asleep on the couch in the next room.

Someone once said, "To err is human. To eat a muskrat is not," but from what I've read on the subject muskrat is pretty tasty. Too bad their mother didn't recognize their good intentions. Instead she went into a silent but pent up rage long enough to not only throw all the muskrat venison into the river, but her iron skillet, too. She switched the legs of all three boys and sent them to bed without any supper. Her children's sobs filled the house and all the commotion woke her husband.

"What the hell," he managed to say before a coughing fit ceased him.

"Those kids were cooking up a muskrat in my

skillet," she told him.

Once he regained his composure he told her, "Swamp bunny is good eatin'. Don't knock it till ye try it, Goldie."

The evening crept by and she made some potato soup, but then began to realize how this kind of living was affecting her kids. She tried praying for help but found her faith was lost. It had been, she realized at that very instant, for a good while. A strong woman like her would find a way to sustain a healthy lifestyle for at least the children – even if she had to compromise her morals to achieve it.

Now Mrs. Goldie Dykes had to make due with what she had. And what she had was a sick husband that couldn't work along with three mischievous well-meaning youngsters to feed, and a fine recipe for what she called "Tap Water." Some fine birch trees resided within walking distance to her house by what locals called the Sluice of the Holston River. What she did was ingenious and no one really knows whether she came up with the recipe on her own or if it was passed down to her by someone who really knew what they were doing. She would "tap" into a birch tree to collect the sap. Once she had a good quantity of the syrup she would mix it with an equal portion of water. Two gallons of the liquid would be added to a gallon of cornmeal within a large stone jar then she set it somewhere warm for three weeks to ferment. Once the fermentation had finished, she drained off the liquid, added a secret ingredient, and poured it into several containers, sealed them, then did something unique to keep them cool for storage. Sworn to secrecy though on what she did. She sold the quarts to whatever trusted soul might mention acquiring some spirited brew. Some might say that Birched Beer is non-alcoholic, but this was simply not true with the Dykes blend. That secret ingredient she added was to zest up the liquid and it had plenty more alcohol content than the 3.2 that was available back during the war.

Ransom Bishop worked up a deal with Goldie Dykes. In exchange for all the "Tap Water" she could produce he would give her extended credit at his store. He would turn around and sell the beverage in back of his shop to some small business owners – and some large ones, too. Fans of the drink called it "Birched Beer". Its true name just never caught on – perhaps for fear of confusion with a bartender who might pour patrons water from the sink.

Suggested Listening: *Possum On A Rail* by The Half-Runners

Cuts

Love thy neighbor as thyself: Do not to others what thou wouldn't not wish be done to thyself: Forgive injuries. Forgive thy enemy, be reconciled to him, give him assistance, invoke God in his behalf.

-Confucius

Roy McClain was one of the Long Island barbers, but he was always said to give the best haircuts anywhere in Kingsport. He also ran a grocery store for a time on the other side of his barber shop.

Most of the rough and tumble on Long Island just called him "Buzz" and most had *mixed it up* with McClain a time or two. It was said many times that Buzz had been whipped by most and whipped a few himself. He was a tall and lean fellow, but wiry and strong and Buzz never backed down from anyone, including the stoutest and toughest brawler on Long Island, Judd Moore.

Once or twice I heard the story of Judd lickin' Buzz pretty bad and throwing him through the front window of Ma Alvis's Restaurant. Because it was pouring rain outside Judd fetched Buzz outside the building and threw him back through the window to keep him from catching a chill.

I am told this fight was because Buzz boasted Judd Moore had backed down from him. On this particular brag – Harry "Hal" Cowden, Judd's good friend, just happened to be the one getting the haircut, so he passed the news along. After confirmation was given him, a sober Judd Moore sought out a drunken Buzz McClain who paid back the transgression first with his hide and then with his pride.

"J-J-Judd. I am sorry," Buzz went on, and he wasn't one to apologize. But his apology was sincere and Judd Moore knew it was.

"Alright then," Judd told him, "You're plenty *worse for wear* now. How 'bout you let me buy you a drink. No hard feelings?"

Honor meant everything on Long Island.

After a drink or four Buzz McClain wished everyone well, and then wandered outside of Ma Alvis's Restaurant. He got into the back of what he thought was a taxi. Nope. It was a police cruiser.

"Ah shit," Buzz exclaimed, seeing Lonzo Morrison, a deputy sheriff, nestled smugly in the driver seat.

"Something you want to tell me Mr. McClain?" the officer asked.

"Yeah," Buzz joked, "Haircuts are on special all this week – buy one get NONE free."

"That's funny, sir," Lonzo smiled, "stayin' out of trouble Buzz?"

"Tryin' my very best, officer. Have a good night."

Buzz tried the handle to get himself out of the vehicle but the door wouldn't budge. It was a rare occasion not to be taken to jail for some trivial offense. The deputy sheriff took Buzz McClain home.

"I'll be in by the next day or so Buzz - due to the special and all."

Then Lonzo Morrison drove away.

The next morning when Opal walked Roger and Debbie to the barber shop to get their hair cut, she had a sneaking suspicion the damage to Roy McClain was her husband's own handy-work based solely on his facial expression as they walked through the door.

Suggested Listening: Settin' The Woods On Fire/ I'll Never Get Out Of This World Alive/Ramblin' Man/Thank God by Hank Williams

Angry Nest

One who is too wise an observer of the business of others, like one who is too curious in observing the labor of bees, will often be stung for his curiosity.

- Alexander Pope

Snapper Jobe pushed hard on the front screen door, sending the screen mesh away from the frame, and reached through, grabbing a revolver that rested on the end table. Then he jumped down the three porch steps of the house, falling onto the sidewalk with a roll, and got up without dusting off. His wobbly pace quickened up the sidewalk and then he stopped by the mail box to raise his weapon.

"MAC - NEW," he cried, "you son-of-a-bitch! I told you to git!" Then he squeezed off a shot.

Barney McNew was across Sixth Street, liquored up, and finding his way home.

"Shit far, Snapper!"

Barney ducked low and spied a pile of bricks laid out by the Brackens' to construct a fine mailbox. Another bullet whizzed passed Barney's grizzled face that snuck through the front window of Mr. Grill's home. By the time Barney McNew scurried to the bricks and claimed one from the arsenal, he had wet himself.

"Wuddint me, Snapper," he called out as he pitched a brick bat like a drunken ballplayer at Snapper Jobe, who was a large man and good sized target. That first block crashed into the mailbox beside Snapper and left a hefty dent. A wasp's nest rested just below the post box and they were plenty riled by the jarring.

All told Barney McNew chucked more than thirteen brick bats as he defended himself from Snapper Jobe, but missed with each throw - sometimes by inches and sometimes totally off the mark. Thank the Good Lord those wasps began stinging Snapper Jobe and messing up his aim. Swearing "Hell fire and blazes" and cussing "F - this, that and you!" he snapped as he fired off the remaining four rounds, then managed to reload with two bullets he'd kept in his front shirt pocket. After dispelling two more awkward shots he hurled the empty revolver at Barney McNew and retreated to the confines of his house like a musk turtle tucked back toward its shell.

The altercation ended in a draw, and the only things hurt were a few feelings, a window, and a rusted out mailbox. The reputation of both men had already been damaged - long before the *Sixth Street Free-for-all*. Jobe and McNew were actually friends most days but when it came to blows on Long Island - and grievances were escalated by the presence of alcohol - scores were settled by extreme measures, even by the best of friends.

Suggested *Listening: The Preacher and the Bear* by Andy Griffith

Taste Buds

We are born believing. A man bears beliefs, as a tree bears apples.
-Ralph Waldo Emerson

Each year, as the blossoming redbud and dogwood trees signal summer's approach, I find my thoughts turning away from today to wander a familiar path back to my Papaw's farm. Summers would find me there as often as allowed, exploring the local woods, roaming my grandfather's orchards and gardens, or trying out my climbing skills on Papaw's favorite apple tree that spread its shade in the back yard.

It seems the days started earlier then with no hardship at all. In the cool of the early morning kitchen, I would sit across the table from my grandfather, Papaw Judd, while my grandmother fixed breakfast. The old man would sit at the kitchen table with a watermelon set squarely on the table before him and his pocketknife open with blade exposed. With some kind of unshared trickery, he would poke the sharp blade into the melon, cut about two inches across it, and right on cue the fruit would split in half with a *thunk*. He would catch me watching with wonderment and grin, then examine the glistening red insides of the fruit. One time he nodded wisely and imparted his secret, "Magic."

Of course I was too wise to be taken in so easily. "Where's your magic hat then?" I asked him.

He leaned back earnestly, jerked his thumb over his left shoulder, and said, "Behind the basement door." My skepticism faltered, and I ran over to the door and opened it. A dusty gray Stetson, the one he wore nearly every day, hung there on a hook.

"It's not so fancy," I observed.

"It don't need to be," he said, adding nonchalantly, "I reckon if you'd like to try some rabbit stew, I could yank the fixins outta that hat by its ears. You'll have to skin it for me, 'course, because I'm kinda busy with this here melon."

I reached up high and took the Stetson off the hook, placed it on top of my small head, and closed the door. Raising my chin, I peeked out from under the hat's wide brim, crossed back to the kitchen table, and sat down.

"What exactly does a rabbit taste like?" I asked.

"A lot like chicken – only more gamey. You want me to pull one out for you to try?"

Although I did like chicken, I quickly answered, "Maybe some other time. Your bein' busy and all."

Looking up to his left at my Mamaw, who had been taking in our entire conversation, he caught her eye, winked, and said, "Yeah, I guess so. Don't reckon you'd want to know what Bugs Bunny really tastes like." Mamaw chuckled and went right on working her own morning culinary magic.

I pushed back that old Stetson in a way I believed looked thoughtful.

"Well, I think I'd want to eat Daffy Duck before I ever ate Bugs Bunny anyway," I declared solemnly, then laughed aloud and repositioned my legs (that nearly touched the floor now) to a sitting position cross-legged on my chair. My Papaw was laughing, too, as he reached across the table and removed the hat from my head before it could fall off. Then he cut me a slice of sweet red fruit.

It was very rare for him to have a bad or unripe watermelon. He had planted the seeds, looked after the vines, tended them as they grew, then somehow knew when to take them from his garden. The same was true for anything he harvested, whether pumpkin, squash, coontail, cucumber, or a variety of beans, peas, or corn. His farming skill stemmed from a kind of knowing you don't acquire from books.

Suggested Listening: *Look Heart, No Hands/Deeper Than the Holler/He Walked on Water/Heroes and Friends* by Randy Travis

The Very Still

Prohibition only drives drunkenness behind doors and into dark places, and does not cure it or even diminish it.

-*Mark Twain*

Ransom Bishop lived at 1612 Island Drive just beside the Sluice. He was a businessman who didn't have to work because he collected a substantial income each month from various sources. His still was all the way across Chigger field and positioned on the Sluice. Actually, the still was across the Sluice and Long Island on Mr. Rodefer's property. Don't worry – the Bishops had to pay a toll and neither Clay Rodefer nor his own father ever went without something to *wet their whistle*. No one would have suspected a burned-out mercantile man like Ransom to be making home brew. But, truth be told, he was the cream of the crop on Long Island. And he was a perfectionist when it came to the taste of his liquor. His still produced a hundred gallons at a time and Bishop sold his product for a wholesale price of around seventy-five cents a half gallon to the Click Brothers. Ransom would run several trout lines out into the Sluice with the containers hooked to the line as well as some fish to keep it legit. Whenever he wanted a quart or twenty he'd bring in whatever was desired and some fish as well for dinner. The street value of a half gallon was more than double that and the Click Brothers couldn't keep it stocked at Club 81 – their rough and tumble underground dive by the bridge on Hwy 81. Club 81 was on private property and signs were everywhere stating "trespassers will be shot on sight." This kept the law away and it discouraged outsiders from Highland, Blair's Gap, and other seedy areas from thinking they could come in unannounced or uninvited.

First and foremost Ransom Bishop was a salesman. It was said among those who had acquaintance with him that he was smooth enough to ball up any religion and sell it back to the church. My Papaw owed him money from a gambling debt and paid him every time the Eastman gave out bonuses. But Ransom had taken advantage of Judd Moore not knowing how to count when he cashed my Papaw's paychecks at week's end. He'd pay a carefree Judd with one dollar bills so it would look as if he was giving a lot back. Once Opal had taught Judd how to count, though, he knew he'd been swindled out of a small fortune. The salesman Ransom could not sell any excuse to Judd Moore and the tension between the two thereafter was evident, though it never came to blows between them.

Now Ransom Bishop, it is said many times over, was clever, *the sharpest knife in the drawer.* And I know writing this might send some rich businessman into a fit but it is the honest truth as I know it to be, and I will share it anyway. Ransom's father was also a pretty smart feller and also a bootlegger and it is believed his father invented a certain drink, passed the recipe on to his son, and Ransom perfected the cocktail – which now has several variations. Long Island, New York would love to take credit for this one and still does to this day – since 1970 as a matter of fact. But as we all know - common people often times aren't recognized for their ingenuity. Invented during Prohibition by Old Man Bishop and perfected by Ransom in the 1940's:

Long Island Iced Tea

One fresh Lemon half
One fresh Lime half

Squeeze both into a pint glass

Add:

½ oz. Rum
1 oz. Vodka
1 oz. Whiskey
½ oz. Gin
½ oz. Tequila
½ oz. Maple Syrup

Mix Thoroughly
Then pour in
4 to 5 oz. Soda Water (Coca-Cola, Pepsi, or RC Cola) without stirring. Enjoy!

Teetotaler drunks have a native Long Island, Tennessean to thank for their alcohol fix. Thank-you Ransom Bishop.

Suggested Listening: *Night Life* by Ray Price

Turkey Run

The meeting of two personalities is like the contact of two chemical substances: if there is any reaction, both are transformed.

-Carl Jung

An off duty Deputy Sheriff named Lonzo Morrison was getting a haircut when he made the mistake of insulting a thirteen year old boy named Kay.

"I'd rather be kin to Hitler himself than be related to those shitass Click Brothers," he had announced in a shop filled with patrons.

The Clicks' young nephew Kay was delivering newspapers on Main Street at a certain barber shop. When the statement was made, he threw one paper in the face of the deputy, then swung his sack around and hit Lonzo hard out of the seat.

"Sorry about this, Mister," he told the barber, "but no

one talks about my family like that."

The law man was beaten senseless. No one was able to pull the lad off Lonzo Morrison, whom didn't even get a lick in. Lonzo had to be carted off to the hospital. News soon spread all over of the fray. The Clicks took notice of their nephew's loyalty and soon put him to work running errands for them on Long Island.

Once he was a young man Kay Gobble worked for his uncles transporting moonshine and bonded liquor from Gate City in Virginia to Long Island in Kingsport, Tennessee. Buck and Zeke Click counted Kay an irreplaceable asset to their trade and they decided to reward him with a brand-new 1949 Hudson Hornet. This was not only so he could outrun the revenuers who gave him chase, but also so he could shave off time with each shipment. Kay treated each mission as a new time to beat and he got really quick at it.

His lead foot proved beneficial for a number of years, but it would eventually prove his demise. One early foggy morning he swerved to miss a school bus and missed a narrow bridge entirely winding up in the river where the twenty-one year old and the Hornet were laid to rest.

Suggested Listening: *Travelin' Blues* by Lefty Frizzell

Varieties

The highest and most lofty trees have the most reason to dread the thunder.

- Charles Rollin

When I was in third grade, my whole science class was required to undertake a difficult assignment collecting thirty or more leaves from different types of trees. Thus was my first Leaf Collection for school. I didn't know where to begin, so I asked my mother for help.

"We'll go to the library and get a book about leaves, then I'll take you up to Bays Mountain and we can find leaves for your project," she had said.

My father had an even better suggestion.

"Why not take Jason over to my parent's house and let him ask my Dad for help? He knows the name of most any tree you could point at from fifty yards away. Besides, there are probably twenty different kinds of trees just in the front and back yard, not to mention the woods."

I agreed that this was a fine idea, and the following weekend my Mom took me to my Papaw's house to ask if he would help me.

"Sure I'll help," he told me, "but you'll have to write

the names down and keep up with the spelling. Do we have a deal?"

The terms defined and unanimously approved, my grandfather and I set out, me with a notebook and pencil in hand. I followed him into the front yard where we gathered our first samples: American Elm, Hickory, Maple, and Weeping Willow. To the back of the house we collected our next specimen, a Chinese chestnut.

"But we aren't in China," I remarked.

"I reckon when the blight went 'n wiped out the American chestnut, the Chinese kinda took over."

This notion was clearly an unhappy one for my Papaw and something of a revelation to me. It wasn't until some years later, however, that I realized the full significance of the American chestnut's demise.

We collected over twenty-five assorted leaves just from trees scattered around the yards of my grandparents' house. Having exhausted this resource, we made our way down through the valley, following the fence line up towards the woods. My Papaw stopped by a fence post and stepped lightly onto some barbed-wire line, carefully lifting the strand above it.

"We'll cross here."

This was the first time I had ever crossed such a boundary and the novelty of it carried a strange mix of excitement and apprehension. I couldn't know that this would be the first of many times I would have to climb through a barbed-wire fence or scale a wall or barrier that designated an arbitrary, manmade division. I have always believed that if God had meant for there to be fences or walls, He would have made them Himself.

There were narrow beaten paths all through the evergreen woodland. This was where deer roamed and hunters went to find them. It was where my cousin Jeff stole his first kiss and a favorite place for the young in the family to play endless games of Hide-n-Seek.

Searching the forest floor of pine needles and leaves, we found five more samples to round out my collection, but my Papaw insisted there was one more tree we needed to visit, just ahead of us a few more yards.

"It is an old tree," he explained, "and this may be the last year it has any leaves."

Soon we stood before a very dark and ugly tree. It rose from a clearing with no other trees near for at least thirty feet. Its trunk was as round as a car tire, but reached only about fifteen feet into the air. A single branch stuck out crookedly, all others having fallen from the tree some time ago. My Papaw picked up a stick the size of a baton and threw it upwards, hitting the branch. A solitary leaf dislodged and seemed to descend in slow motion. I lifted my arms to capture it, but my Papaw caught it just above my reach.

"This is a very special tree," he informed me before handing over the browning leaf. "It was once tall and strong; the most beautiful tree in all these woods. Then one dark night a bolt of lightnin' struck it down, leaving what you see right here. I'd meant to come out here years ago with my saw and put it out of its misery."

I examined the leafy specimen in my hand, but could find nothing special about it compared with the other samples I had already collected. Placing it into my notebook, I asked, "What kind is it?"

My grandfather leaned up against the tree, squatted a little, and then pushed off with his legs. The tree leaned away from him, hung there a moment, and then swayed back, though not all the way. He spun around, placed his right foot against the trunk about three feet above the ground, and leaned into the tree. The force of his push shifted it forward; there was a cracking noise from somewhere deep in the dying wood. "Help me push this," he said. I stepped up beside him and pushed on the tree with my small hands. The trunk cracked again, and then gave way all together, toppling to earth in a sudden, single motion. A roaring sound accompanied its descent, and my Papaw lifted me up and away from the path of its fall. Upon impact with the ground, the decaying timber splintered into several pieces.

My Papaw set me down and studied our handiwork. "What did you ask me again?" he questioned.

I was staring in wonder at the tree's shattered remains. It took me a moment to gather my thoughts.

"What kind of tree was it?"

"Oh yes," He frowned a little and nodded, "it's what we mountain folk like to call a Rotted Oak," he replied.

I asked him to help me spell "Rotted" but he reminded me of our deal, "You keep up with the spelling and stuff. I'll provide the names."

As we hiked back from the woodland, my Papaw was very silent. I ran on ahead and waited by the barbed-wire fence where we had crossed over. He approached slowly, like he was too busy turning something over in his mind to hurry much. Before ducking on through the barrier, he said something that has stuck with me throughout my life.

"I reckon trees are a lot like people."

I saw his eyes were looking far off to somewhere only his mind could see as he tried to explain.

"There's all kinds. It ain't about color either. That's just outside. It's more about the fruits or nuts they yield and how well they make it in the world."

He looked down to me thoughtfully.

"You understand?"

"Kind of," I said, trying to fit his words into the day's events. "Now is a Rotted Oak pretty rare?"

As an adult, I have come to realize that my Papaw's observation holds many truths, even beyond those he had explained. Like he then noted - there are many varieties of tree in on the earth and there are many kinds of people in this world. Some are like sprouts that never quite make it beyond the first few years of existence, while others grow tall and strong with age. Some bear much fruit whether it is in the Biblical sense of having offspring, or in the worldly sense of producing wealth or accumulating material goods. Each tree, in its differences, has something to contribute. Trees seem to know this, as do most things in nature. Only man seems confused by the concept. If trees could impart their ancient wisdom, I often wonder if humankind would listen or understand.

What we make of life and how well we survive its lightning strikes is what truly matters.

Suggested Listening: My *Tennessee Mountain Home*/Everything's Beautiful(In It's Own Way) by Dolly Parton and Willie Nelson

Fruits and Nuts

Dieu me pardonnera. C'est son métier. (God will forgive me. It's his job)

-Heinrich Heine

Like starving dogs the kids would show up outside the Moore home place on McKinney Street. The Moore family had the biggest yard to play in and the woods were conveniently located close by. Dwight Conklin lived just next door. J.C. Frazier resided across the street. Jerry Taylor was close, too. The Davenports had seven kids. Pastor Collins had five children. They lived on Happy Hill. The Bowens lived just a few streets over on Oaklawn and they contributed another five kids to the community. Their eldest son Hoyt was new to my father's circle of friends and Roger Moore made sure he fit right in with the existing crowd. The boys in Springdale formed sort of a brotherhood. They were like brothers in many ways. Roger was always making sure no one picked on Hoyt.

"Mess with him and you're messing with me," he advised anyone who needed it - friend or foe. Mrs. Moore would always invite Hoyt inside and insist he help himself to some breakfast. He always declined at first then would get talked into a slice or two of bacon. Hoyt Bowen's family was of adequate means and his own mother made sure he had eaten breakfast before she let him go out to play.

"Bring your friends here once and a while so I can have a look at them," Mrs. Bowen instructed him whenever he shot out the front door and down the steps like a bullet. In no time at all the whelp of a youngster was nearly as big as any kid his age.

As the days turned to months and months to years Roger and Hoyt became the very best of friends. They were inseparable. They rode their bicycles all over Springdale. Hoyt was no longer the puny kid new to the neighborhood and he became known somewhat as a prankster – always telling jokes – making up funny stories – and teasing pretty girls. He was quite an athlete, too.

An up-in-years farmer named Mr. Eads once commissioned Hoyt and Roger to rid his farm of a wild cat. This old cat had the run of the neighborhood and terrorized the community – but it paid special attention to Mr. Eads' place.

"Drown that varmint in this here pond. That menace has kilt ev'ry one of my chicks this year. It's a gol-dern nuisance."

When most folks think about cats they think about the cute and fluffy domesticated creatures seen on commercials for *Meow Mix* but - truth be told – solid gold - there are more wild felines than tame ones. And this young cat was one tough customer. The farmer had shot at that cat any time it showed itself to him, but – try as he might – the varmint was either lucky or bulletproof.

"Thought I'd got that rascal with my 12 gauge once,"

he explained, "but – when I went to recover his body – there was no sign of injury – other than my wife's favorite holly bush."

He was troubled by the predicament and the boys all waited for him to continue.

"Damn huntin' dog won't get him," he went on, shaking his head, "Zane Grey here just lays out on the porch all day and won't ev'n acknowledge the postman. In fact, I kept Zane's food on the back porch for a long time and thought I heard that cat rustlin' around in there, so I grabbed up my shovel and whacked the package a few times. The awfullest odor ye ever smelt come steamin' outta that bag. Wouldn't ye know it – I kilt a polecat. I had to bury that whole bag of dog food and that skunk and take me a bath in tomato juice to get that smell off me."

"We'll rid your farm of that monster, sir," Hoyt assured Mr. Eads, "and any other *scaled-down piece of evil* you see fit for us to destroy, too."

Roger and Hoyt had done quite a bit of work for this up-in-years farmer in the past -every type of chore from cleaning out the chicken coop and putting up hay or planting corn – just whatever Mr. Eads would determine them to do. Pest control was by no means out of the question either.

The boys devised a plan to capture the beast alive, but soon found that the ferocious feline was a clever trickster. After several traps failing to work or having their patience tried to the maximum level – they both began to feel like Wiley Coyote twins trying to snag the Roadrunner.

"Dang puss has survived this long," Hoyt managed, "maybe we are meant to fail on this one Roger. Hmm."

"Well, Mr. Eads has our word and I'm not giving up

until his farm has been eradicated of that no good demon. Hold on," Roger gestured suddenly in a whisper, motioning in the direction of the chicken coop. The cat snuck around the corner of the coop and was preparing to pounce on one of the farmer's hens. The boys were quiet – careful not to alarm the creature as each bent low and picked up a good-sized river stone. Hoyt looked to Roger as each boy drew back, then Roger nodded and the boys each hurled the projectiles and... WHAM!

Reow!

That cat got hit in mid pounce and it spun around in the air and did a face plant into the earth.

"Got him! We got him! I told you," Hoyt nudged Roger in the ribs then put his arm around Roger into a headlock.

"Sure as sugar is sweet and the sun is still shining – that daggum varmint is history."

The cat suddenly came to and collected its bearings as it arose on all fours and shook itself off before looking around, then – like a bottle rocket – shot up then forward but ran with a burst of speed headfirst into the trunk of a Cedar tree. It fell away dazed and Roger reached down and grabbed the feline by the back of its neck. The cat gave a jerk and wriggled some but couldn't get free or turn to dig its blood-stained claws into the boy. It then gave a pissed-off warning that sounding like a fire engine siren starting to whine – the kind of noise two tomcats will make when vying for the affection of a pussycat in heat.

The boys followed Mr. Eads instructions *to the letter* in

drowning the nuisance. Hoyt and Roger hog-tied the hissing monster's legs together with some twine. Then they used the extra length of twine to connect the deadly cat to a large river rock. Wouldn't you know it? That trickster was the feline Houdini and worked some underwater magic, freeing itself from its bondage and swimming to shore. The boys had to wrestle that feline into a potato sack and secure it snug before pitching the varmint back into the pond where its life must have finally expired.

The farmer was so pleased with Roger and Hoyt's determination and resolve he paid the boys a dollar each. The average wage at Tennessee Eastman at that time was thirty-five cents an hour. So – one can imagine how proud they were to be of service.

Legend has it the trickster cat shape-shifted into a mutated mud-turtle because an enormous mud-turtle, possibly an Alligator Snapper, was the notorious nuisance thereafter, drowning ducklings and often swallowing fishing lures whole. Mr. Eads would drain the pond every year for the sole purpose of finding that killer creature and ridding his haunted farm of the evil cat's spirit once and for all. I've walked the pasture and down to where the pond once was. It's dried up now, but `there lays a mammoth shell imbedded in the earth covered with ivy now. It looks like a monolith turned over and half buried. I have stood upon the back of this beast. I believe it is a raven now who has found its mate. You might see this trickster sometime – if you'll only look for him.

Suggested Listening: Mean Eyed Cat/Dirty Old Egg-Sucking Dog/Country Trash/The Man Comes Around/ Dark As A Dungeon/Father and Son by Johnny Cash

Peanuts

When a man tells you that he got rich through hard work, ask him: 'Whose?'

Don Marquis

An Eastman foreman had a large Bull pine fall down onto his fence one time and the cows were getting loose and wandering out into the neighborhood. The foreman had a younger son (who later became a banker) he had charged with supervision of the farm, and the son decided to hire some of the Springdale boys to clean up the mess. The Davenports, Eddie and Johnny, and Roger Moore were the ones he put to work. They were all in their early teens in age but used to farm labor, mending fences and putting up hay. But this was no ordinary chore. The boys had to use a cross-cut saw and some clever ingenuity to remove the tree and clear the brush away. Then they had to round up all of the cows. Roger's dog King was now fully grown and he helped the boys locate and herd in the cattle. It took the boys more than half of the day before the foreman's son was satisfied and ready to pay the boys.

Later that evening when Judd Moore returned home

from a long day at the coal pile he asked his son Roger, "How long did it take you?"

"Eight hours or so."

"What did he pay you?"

Roger reached into his denim pants pocket and produced a quarter.

Judd waved the quarter away and shook his head in disapproval.

"You should have told him to stick it up his ass," his father advised him.

If I was to ask some politician or corporate bureaucrat from this contemporary circus of no-goods what hard work is, I wonder what their answer would be. Is it pausing while on vacation for a photo opportunity beside a brand new pick-up truck? Image is everything, right? But why paint up some façade? Why not roll up the shirtsleeves and get the hands dirty – clean out the stables themselves for once? Why not? I will tell you why. The silver spoon that rests shiny in their mouth says they've never had to. If I was to ask that same politician to explain to me why their salary has been increased by at least thirty thousand dollars the past ten years and their health benefits are complimentary and never ending – and will continue even after they leave office – at the taxpayer's expense – I wonder how they might explain that. And how might they justify never increasing the minimum wage for over a decade? And Mr. Big Business Mogul -what about the continued increase of healthcare and gasoline? I'd love to know why this is. Actually, I know why it is. Every free thinker in America should know why. And it isn't just that no one in Washington D.C. or Corporate America gives a damn about the common person who shovel out that crap that only make the rich even richer. They do toss out those peanuts for us to all eat. It is strange though, elephants not liking peanuts. There is an old saying: With great power comes great responsibility. And there is another: Absolute power corrupts absolutely. The next time a corrupt politician or Jihad extremist invokes God in a speech – remind yourself of these verses from the Bible: II Thessalonians 2:8-12.

Sorry for the rambling. Hard work here in east Tennessee is something far different than any photo opportunity.

Suggested Listening: *Working for the Man* by Roy Orbison

Red Skin Green Skin

There are some things, which cannot be learned quickly, and time, which is all we have, must be paid heavily for their acquiring. They are the very simplest things, and because it takes a man's life to know them the little new that each man gets from life is very costly and the only heritage he has to leave.

- Ernest Hemingway

Throughout recorded history - perhaps even from the dawn of our species - mankind has regarded differences with suspicion and fear, or settled them with fists, sharpened steel, the squeeze of a trigger, and the push of a button. Perhaps this is what separates us from most other life forms. However civilized a history book may claim the modern human race to be, the veneer is thin and we are ultimately still savage in nature. On the larger scale of settling disputes, war is usually the beaten path to resolution.

War is often times a senseless slaughter of carnage brought forth by bureaucrats and businessmen who, themselves, never had to serve a single day of combat. Sometimes war is justified. As Joseph Campbell noted *"The battlefield"* really *"is symbolic of the field of life, where every creature lives on the death of another…"*

My Papaw, Judd Moore, was twenty-three when the United States officially entered World War II. In mid-October of 1942, on the day he turned twenty-four years of age, he received his draft notice via telegram. He broke the news to Opal Hayes, the pretty lady destined - for better or worse - to be my Mamaw while they picked blackberries in a field near her father's house. He thought it only fair as he was planning to follow up immediately with a proposal of marriage. Opal promptly and joyously accepted, despite the fact that her father had already flatly withheld his permission. Uncle Sam had left Judd no more time to win Martin Hayes' paternal blessing, so he and Opal decided to elope. One week after they wed, Judd Moore boarded a bus that would take him to Fort Oglethorpe, Georgia and Basic Training.

Although he was not happy to be forced into the role of soldier, my grandfather went with his head held high. However, drill sergeants and instructors could and did say anything they saw fit to break a person down, and would resort to physical abuse of a trainee if verbal abuse was not working. This type of free reign with authority was something Judd Moore never took very well. A stiff spine in combination with the short fuse on his temper could only mean trouble for someone. It was just a matter of time.

That time came on his third day in the United States Army, when a screaming drill sergeant called him a son of a bitch. For Judd, it was pure reflex upon being called anything - let alone a stranger disrespecting his mother. He lunged forward, tackled the instructor around the waist, and then went to work on him with his fists until the other sergeants were able to pull him off. They restrained Judd against a wall, one man holding him on either side, while the battered instructor punched him repeatedly in the stomach. When at last they felt his pride had suffered enough, they released Judd's arms and let him fall face first onto the concrete. It was a hard start to his training as a soldier.

In the weeks that followed, further discipline of that sort was not needed. Judd learned not to take everything the sergeants said so personally. Soon, his physical abilities, work ethic, and marksmanship skills earned him the respect of his peers and instructors alike. In fact, he and one instructor, Sergeant Yates, in time became good friends.

Though my Papaw never learned to read or write, Opal wrote regularly. Sergeant Yates would read these welcome and loving letters aloud to Judd, then take down Judd's reply word for word. He taught Judd Moore how to write his name. The finished letters could then be signed and folded into an envelope, to be mailed to Green Shed where Opal was staying with a family by the name of Hooks. She was both surprised and pleased to receive the first letter he had ever sent her, and thereafter looked forward to each and every one.

"He always said very nice things to me in those letters," she once told me.

A decade or so after World War II ended, the Korean conflict erupted and drafting again took place. A decade later, in the '60s, young men throughout the United States were being drafted into the Armed Services to settle political differences in far-off Vietnam. These young men came from all over, including Kingsport, Tennessee and the Springdale community. It was my father, Roger Moore's turn to serve. He had always been very patriotic and prideful of the American Way, so, unlike my Papaw, he didn't wait to be drafted. He felt it his duty as an American to enlist himself even before his senior year of high school had ended. He was Judd Moore's only son.

"Why did you go and do that?" The question had to be asked. Judd had seen war.

"Well, Daddy," Roger answered, "I just feel like it's the right thing to do."

Judd stated the heart of the truth he feared. "You'll get yourself killed."

Roger had been *bitten by the love bug* for his last two years of high school. His sweetheart and first love was a lovely jewel across town in Lynn Garden named Barbara. She was a few years younger than he was and she, too, didn't necessarily agree with his decision to enlist in the United States Army while the war in Vietnam was at a boiling point.

Roger shook Judd Moore's hand at the bus station and his father gripped his hand like he would have any man, then released it kind of slow. Then his father gave a nod and walked away from him before he could see the tears welling up in his eyes. Roger hugged his girlfriend Barbara good-bye and she was crying.

"Be safe. And come home to me," she managed.

He handed her an envelope, winked, and then boarded the bus for Fort Jackson, South Carolina.

> Here I am in my fatigues though I don't look too well as usual but this picture will help remind you of me during your lovely tours when we're apart. Someday in the future we'll be together forever but till then we'll just have to wait. Until then always remember that I love you with all my heart. Love ya Roger

Herodotus said, *"In peace sons bury their fathers. In war fathers bury their sons."*

By grace, my father served his country well and he survived. His mental scars were many – and cut him deep and to his core foundations. His service in Vietnam made him question the things he'd been taught in church, school, and his upbringing. No matter the answer it is good to question things. Blind faith in a certain belief can lead a man off a cliff edge.

Though I, too, would ultimately join the U.S. Army during the first Gulf War as a military policeman - by no means would I even consider comparing myself to them.

Dad always told me the heroes were those men that never came back. I never believed that. He came home, as did my grandfather, and I have had the privilege of knowing them both.

In my eyes, both of them are heroes.

Suggested Listening: *All Along The Watchtower/Foxey Lady/Voodoo Child/Machine Gun/Star Spangled Banner* by Jimi Hendrix

In Passing

Courage, it would seem, is nothing less than the power to overcome danger, misfortune, fear, injustice, while continuing to affirm inwardly that life with all its sorrows is good; that everything is meaningful even if in a sense beyond our understanding; and that there is always tomorrow.

Dorothy Thompson

I had a great uncle named Don Light that I only got to know through stories. Don was a veteran of the Korean War. His favorite actor was Steve McQueen, the *King of Cool*. Don was always cracking jokes and playing pranks on people, but he was considerate of others, too. Don often said the blessing at the dinner table.

"Good food. Good meat. Good God, let's eat. *Amen.*"

He drove a race car and was a crowd favorite locally at the Kingsport International Speedway where he developed quite a following driving a 68' Ford in the late 1960's and early 1970's - once finishing as high as seventh in the point standings. He had three children – Todd, Penny, and Aaron. My cousin Aaron was only three years old in July of 1976 when his father Don was killed instantly at age 41 when a bobtail tractor in which he was a passenger veered out of control and smashed into a roadside dumpster. Aaron learned stories about his father Don as he grew into a man and these stories helped him become a man himself his father would be most proud of.

Don Light's nephew Corporal Robbie Light went proudly to serve his country in far off Iraq on his first tour of duty from 2003 to 2004. Based at Fort Hood, Texas, with C Company, 1-67 Armor Division, 2nd Brigade of the 4th Infantry Division, he would return to Iraq for a second tour of duty in 2005, this time leaving his wife Elizabeth with a pooching stomach. Robbie was photographed caressing his pregnant wife Elizabeth's belly before leaving on this second deployment. Corporal Light lost his life on May 1 of 2006 when an improvised explosive device (IED) detonated near the M1-A2 Abrams tank he was driving in Baghdad. He was a model soldier, a mere twenty-one years old and a father himself, but his daughter Ashlyn was born five days before her Dad was laid to rest in June 2006.

Today - as I write this I am reminded how precious life is and I say a prayer for this little girl - I pray that stories of her father's courage will echo through the walls and halls of her home growing up - and she will know who her father was through these stories.

I have a daughter myself whom I would slay a dragon for any day. Robbie would have done the same for his daughter Ashlyn.

Suggested Listening: *Steve McQueen/Redemption Day/No Depression In Heaven* by Sheryl Crowe, *Angel Band/A Beautiful Life* by the Stanley Brothers

DISSIPATE

Detached from the things that are seen
I feel and hear my heart like a drum
Struck soft in my chest granting me life
Springing up like a flower to the sun.
It beats ever soft like a youth
Pounding slowly then faster I fear
As a vision enters the threshold and
The flower drops slow like a tear.
Endless wasteland – disappear.

Drums in the distance beat wildly.
Inside my chest there is a child in control
Sending rhythms that pulsate the wall like
Slants of light from the sun through my soul.
Illuminant mysteries are surrounding
Powers that are unseen by my eyes
As the dreaded dream a nightmare it seems
Touches the very mask of disguise.
Existence rooted up. Vitality dies.

Dead are the things I have seen
In a world where the garden is bare
Solemn yet bringing no life
Seeds from the depths of despair.
I am the one who went walking out
Planting my heart as I went.
As the drumbeat settles in failure
The flowers spring up to repent.
Ethereal garden. Glorious scent.

Suggested Listening: *Civil War/Patience* by Guns and Roses

Pardon Me

I can forgive, but I cannot forget, is only another way of saying, I will not forgive. Forgiveness ought to be like a canceled note -- torn in two, and burned up, so that it never can be shown against one.

-Henry Ward Beecher

Harry "Hack" Cleek was caught running shine in the early Forties and had to spend one year and a day at a penitentiary in Chillicothe, Ohio. Hack shot an ABC man a few months after his release and spent some time in the federal pen in Kentucky then he was transferred to a roughest place he'd ever seen, The Nashville State prison. But after World War II erupted a twenty-four year old Hack went before the magistrate who gave him the option of spending the remainder of his years in prison or serving the United States military in Europe. He chose Option B and was shipped out to Fort Meade, Kentucky for Combat Engineer training. The prison in Nashville was a cakewalk compared to the things he would see in combat.

During *The Battle of the Bulge* Hack was driving a bulldozer across the Rhine Valley clearing a roadway where the bombs had cratered the ground when he looked across his right shoulder and saw his younger brother Bill charging ahead, bullets whizzing past them both, men falling around them. Seeing his brother still alive rejuvenated his spirits because he'd been worried for Bill since they'd parted ways many months earlier. Hack had orders for the South Pacific but "Fat Man" and "Little Boy" ended the war before he was shipped out from Europe to Asia. After the war ended Hack was a seasoned and decorated war hero, earning the Bronze Star for his bravery, and in 1946 President Harry S. Truman pardoned Harry B. Cleek, absolving him of his wrongdoings.

Upon his release Hack determined with his new lease on life he had earned this freedom with what he'd seen and done in the war and decided it best to straighten himself up for good. His wife Margaret informed him she couldn't stay with him if he kept breaking the law. And he loved her and he loved their children like a child loves candy. Margaret Clark was his sweetheart.

He kept his nickname, of course, like Sir Gawain wore the green belt as a reminder. He worked for the Holston Ordinance and the Tennessee Valley Authority, and since retiring served Sullivan County since 1974 as the Sullivan Gardens Fire Department Chief to the day he left this old world. Last time I met with Hack was at L.E. Clark's Grocery in Sullivan Gardens. I had my daughter Bethany with me and he told her some interesting stories. I could tell he loved kids when I saw his interaction with her. At eighty-eight years of age he was still as colorful and talkative as ever. The last thing he said to me was "I haven't seen Clay Rodefer in years. Ask him to come and see me. Will you?" When I did see Clay Rodefer a week later I passed the message along to him and he had already paid his old friend a visit. You see Hack Cleek passed away three days after I'd spoken to him in June of 2006. And Clay came to say his good-byes at the funeral home.

Hack was definitely one of the good guys and will be greatly missed. It was an honor meeting with him this past year.

Stop in sometime at Clark's Grocery off Highway 93 and order a Big Hack burger of choice – the very best burgers in Kingsport – and pay your respects.

Suggested Listening: If Teardrops Were Pennies/A Satisfied Mind/ Green, Green Grass of Home/Always, Always *by Porter Wagoner and Dolly Parton*

Ripe

If you have an apple and I have an apple and we exchange these apples then you and I will still each have one apple. But if you have an idea and I have an idea and we exchange these ideas, then each of us will have two ideas.

George Bernard Shaw

My brother Kevin and I both grew up being called *"the Moore Boys"* by most who knew us. But, truth is, my brother and I both were born with our mother's maiden name - Carter - which was quite a famous last name. My Grandpa on my mother's side was a second cousin to June Carter of the famous Carter

Family which made us related by marriage to Johnny Cash as well. However distant, I have never met my famous cousins or any of the Carter or Cash family either. And although I always thought it would be quite a meeting of the minds and the music it was never pursued any more than just daydreaming when I was in grade school.

Kevin was nine days shy of being one year older than I am. We were both born in January, and astrologically I am part goat and he is a water-bearing fairy. We differ greatly - in other words. My brother has always watched out for me throughout my life. Even now he makes sure I'm not causing trouble or being harassed. My mother drew welfare and made due with what little we had during my first two years of existence, and then something happened: she was introduced to one of my Grandmother Jean's good friends, Roger Moore. Vickie Carter began to date him. He was a veteran of the Vietnam War, a hard worker, and a very respectful man. Like his father Judd Moore - Roger was employed at Tennessee Eastman.

Soon after my mother and Roger Moore met, they were married.

Although Roger had no children, he was more than happy to adopt us two boys as his own. In his own father's eyes at the time, Judd felt grieved by his only son Roger taking two bastard youngsters under his arm as family.

Truth is – one of the first things Roger did when he left the United States Army was get a vasectomy.

"What the damn hell are you thinkin' son? Shit far – what about having kids of yer own?" Judd asked.

"I'll adopt."

From an older, traditional, standpoint of thinking, I can understand his old man's belief about this.

However, the worldview of my Dad, Roger Moore, has a more agreeable outlook than Judd Moore could have realized at first. For Example, Kevin and I legally entered into the Moore family each at an early age and like rearing a puppy or a kitten it's usually a good thing. This way we were not so wild going in, no biting or hissing, scratching, or barking. We were ready to love, taught to be respectful, and disciplined as needed - even if Judd Moore growled at us a little in the beginning.

The funniest thing, though, is that Judd Moore was technically not a Moore at all, but a Horton. His father Martin had taken the Moore name when he was still a young man, to hide some lawbreaking record I am certain. It wasn't too hard to become someone else back then.

The worldview of my father changed after he went to Vietnam. Wherever the American military has been, there are orphans. The truth of the matter is whether it is Vietnam or Korea or other parts of Asia a child fathered by an American soldier has no rights to citizenship in their own country. Having seen countless children without parents, Roger Moore decided there are enough kids in the world without their fathers. Why bring more into it?

Suggested Listening: *This Old Road/For The Good Times/To Beat The Devil/The Pilgrim: Chapter 33* By Kris Kristopherson

BUSHELS

Security is mostly a superstition. It does not exist in nature....
Life is either a daring adventure or nothing.

- Helen Keller

On July 3rd, 1976, the day before the great Bicentennial Parade of Kingsport, we gathered around the front porch of the Moore home place at 1829 McKinney Street.

"It was really nice meeting you Mrs. Moore," my mother said her right hand on my brother's left shoulder, leading him off the porch.

"You, too.   You, too," Opal replied with her reassuring way of saying things and a genuine nod.

I was sitting up on Roger Moore's shoulders out in

the yard. He was hopping around like the Easter Bunny. Easter being the last holiday I'd remembered at two and a half years old we were seeking out invisible eggs, but found a discolored one his niece or nephew hadn't found or claimed months earlier. I wanted to hold it, but he explained that it was rotten and was not fit for his Daddy's old Norwegian Elkhound, Pepper, to eat.

"Yuck," he had said.

"Yuck," I echoed from just above him.

"Yuckity Yuck," my brother chimed in from the porch-step.

About this time an apple red '71 Dodge drove slowly along the road in front of the house, and then pulled down into the driveway stopping in front of a rickety tool-shed. The truck tires along the gravel drive sounded like a worn out Sherman Tank steadily advancing upon Rommel's forces in North Africa. Judd Moore sat in the cab of his truck wrapping one of his newly prized pocketknives with a napkin. Then he leaned to the passenger side placing it into the glove compartment and shut the hatch. He swung open the driver side door and stepped out slow with about an inch of cigar still in the side of his mouth. His look was proud like that of an army general but his was a different kind of pride. A man troubled. Torn. I could sense his mood from that distance even at such a young age.

"C'mon around here and be sociable," Roger's mother called out to him.

He grumbled, extinguished the cigar, and then set it on the dashboard for later. He stood holding the driver side door with it still ajar like he had forgotten something. But what? Roger slid me carefully down his back to the soft grass, gave me a wink and smile, then walked over to his father by the Dodge. I sat there alongside Pepper, his father's dog, and immediately got distracted by the old pooch licking the side of my face. My brother laughed and ran from my mother's grips toward the dog and me. We play wrestled together with Pepper as my mother and Opal found places to sit down on the porch.

"These things take time," Roger's mother assured her, "They do. The Good Lord broke the mold after He made Judd Moore."

"My boys really love your son," my mother told her with confidence.

"That matters to a degree Vickie, but it's you who he's marrying. Those two rascals are a bonus." Opal advised her.

"You mean rug-rats?" my mom asked her.

"Is that what he calls them?" Mrs. Moore laughed, "Judd will come around. You just be sure this is what you want for yourself, and your two... um... rug-rats."

"I know," my mother responded, "and I will."

Suggested Listening: *Don't Let Me Cross Over* by Carl Butler and Pearl

MOTHER

My mother means to me
    the beginning and warmth of Spring
Obtaining the rays of sunlight
    to nourish most everything
Trust in her love has given me
    the strength to rise up from the earth
Her support has radiated my heart
    like a flower with bud in full birth
Evening shadows may find me
    as raindrops aplenty revive
Replenish my spirit with sustenance
    and helping to always survive.

-JS Moore

Without my Grandmother Jean Brown introducing Roger Moore to my mother – I might have never known the man. He might have been someone I exchanged a glance with - who passed by me at the package store on his way to get some peppermint schnapps or Wild Irish Rose. He might have stopped by the roadside to help me fix a flat. It is always difficult not to ask 'what if?' I cannot fathom what my life or my brother's life would have been like without the influence of Roger and his family. The full significance of this one connection, this one introduction removed from my life, and I would have been someone else - definitely not be who I've become. Since I've become a father she's been telling me, "There are only a handful of things a person should be asked to fight for: Our self dignity, our God, but the main one – the first one – is our children." Isn't that right?

Something my great grandmother Paul Brown always taught her children was: If stranded on a deserted island, you might have to suffer some – but you would learn to survive without depending on others for help. This isn't pride, but responsibility. I believe our leaders and business owners should reexamine their outside investments. We shouldn't depend on other countries for cheap labor. We shouldn't move our factories overseas to keep from having to follow environmental regulations or paying fair wages. These businesses have inadvertently built the perfect beast, and gradually we Americas have lost our respect all over the world. Doing what is right isn't always easy. And doing what is easy isn't always right. Right? For our society to support itself it will have to be able to sustain itself without all this dependence overseas. Our children will be left with our mistakes to correct. They will have to suffer even more than we have. Let's fix this now.

It's funny really – to say in this day and age we've lost step with how things once were… that *The Good Old Days* are behind us. But it is doing our history an injustice to even think it. Things were just as bad then as they are now. It's true. It's just our history books whitewash the facts. About the time I was being born a fine lady named Mary Conklin, Opal and Judd Moore's neighbor, wrote this letter to the Editor of the Kingsport Times News:

Is *the* democracy?

A democracy is a government "of the people, by the people, for the people," isn't it? So what do we call the form of government we now have? The people had nothing to do with electing the president or vice-president. One of them had already been turned down by the people more than once.

Why weren't the people allowed to vote on it? There was an election in November. It would have saved time, money, and most important it would have given the people a choice.

The 93rd Congress could have been working on the important problems and perhaps had something to pat themselves on the back about besides ousting a president elected by the people and cleaning up the most corrupt administration in history. That's pure speculation since it's the only one they had ever investigated.

Watergate was important only to the politicians and the press. All the months they were keeping it in the news, the American public was worrying about other problems that no one was doing anything about. This country didn't get into the condition it's in overnight. Were they using the Watergate Scandal to cover up their inabilities to cope with the economic problems?

In the last few months we have been getting "shock treatments" from the news in almost every edition. One day we were told we were the richest nation in the world, the next that we didn't have anything. That must have been the greatest burglary in history.

I would like to hear something about some one at least trying to do something about high prices, shortages, and unemployment. The American people don't want "handouts."

We have promises that they will do something, they don't know what. Sometime they don't know when promises made last week are broken this week. Promises of politicians remind me of snowflakes melting before they hit the ground. They aren't enough, are they?

- Mary Conklin
1825 McKinney St.

Looking over her letter – I see many issues that parallel the problems and challenges we are facing today.

Suggested Listening: *I Hope You Dance* by LeeAnn Womack

ROTTEN

"It is remarkable how closely the history of the apple tree is connected with that of man."

-Henry David Thoreau

My parents' relationship was good for a while but eventually it went bad. Eight years after Roger Moore and Vickie Carter wed - they divorced. It was finalized on my mother's birthday in 1985. It was what she wanted.

Kevin and I arrived at my Grandparents one early spring Saturday just as the sun was waking up in the Tennessee sky. The tool shed was empty. Papaw's truck was gone. My Dad led us boys onto the concrete porch to the front door. As we waited for my Mamaw to come to the door I caught sight of a marking in the porch I hadn't noticed before. It was a date etched into the cement that was nearly 30 years old. I took a mental note of the marking as the front door came open and my brother and I were guided inside.

"Kevin," my Mamaw spoke up, "I've made you some pancakes – special – just for you. And Jason, I have a box of Cocoa Pebbles with your name all over it."

"I'm not so hungry," I shrugged.

Kevin had already gone into the kitchen and was helping himself to his favorite breakfast. I often teased my brother that his stomach was a bottomless pit for he could eat for hours and hours by the plateful without getting fat or sick. I was a much pickier eater than my brother. It was well known by most who knew me that chocolate was my favorite food. But this sullen day I didn't feel too much like eating anything.

"Go into the kitchen, Jason," my father encouraged, "your Mamaw and I need to talk."

Although I very much wanted to hear what they had to say, I knew it was none of my business – and so I pouted my way into the kitchen.

"Hey there Yogi Bear," my thirteen-year-old cousin Tammy hollered out.

"Hey," I answered lowly, "what are you doing here?"

"Well, what does it look like I'm doin? I'm having myself one heckuva egg sandwich. Mm umm good," she countered.

Suddenly my worries left me and I played along with my cousin's friendly banter.

"I don't see no picnic basket, Boo Boo," I remarked filling an empty seat at the table.

Engrossed in Cocoa Pebbles and conversation with my cousin and brother I never even heard my father go out the front door to the truck. I never even heard him come back in again with our luggage. My mother had stayed at our house to pack up her things. She hadn't come with us because she would have not been so strong. She had a tendency to cry just about anytime she would be without Kevin and me for more than a few days. This would be for much longer, though. With the impending divorce - a mutual agreement was made between my parents that *"the Moore Boys"* would stay with Judd and Opal Moore to finish out the school year at Sullivan Elementary School.

It doesn't matter that their union was for a mere eight years and ended in divorce. It doesn't matter that with the split my brother and I – soon after - moved away with our mother to Rogersville, Tennessee, thirty plus miles away from our Dad. What matters is Roger Moore loved us boys enough to remain in our lives, continue to help shape us into men, and he became the best father two mongrel boys could ever wish for.

After a few hours of playing assorted games and drawing pictures with my brother Kevin and my cousin Tammy I stepped into the kitchen and asked my Mamaw about the date etched onto the front porch. She told me a story about my Papaw, which I wanted to hear more of – in every detail. Later on I asked my Dad to tell me about the date etched in the porch – May 29, 1955.

Suggested Listening: *Candy Apple Red* by Tom Waits

From early childhood to adolescence, I had watched my Papaw Judd, listened to his stories, and learned from him. The most memorable times were when he shared with me stories that no one else really knew.

I picture him now, settled down on the porch after supper on a warm summer evening – a large, red apple in one hard, calloused hand, pocketknife in the other – engaging in the precise ritual of dissecting that Red Delicious while he talked and I listened. The continuous strand of very thin, crimson skin would descend little by little, spiraling down onto a plate – like a slinky - each time he would shave away the peeling.

Throughout my life I have attempted to do the same, but get no further than a few short inches of thick skin, maybe less, when a shaving falls away and my failure as a Pomology surgeon ruins the procedure. I remember watching him examine the fruit for any sign of rot or bruise to cut away as he moved the razor-sharp blade along the surface of the apple. He had mastered this art within the seventy-three years God gave him, and I never once saw the skin fall when he did not want it to.

My father did, though.

Breaking the Skin

Accident, n.: A condition in which presence of mind is good, but absence of body is better.

Ambrose Bierce

One Saturday in the late spring of '55, before the old rooster called out to the rising blaze of dawn, Judd Moore awoke to a hangover and an empty house. Sitting silent at the foot of the bed, he slid on his denim Big Mac overalls, then his socks and leather work boots. Thirty-five, fit and muscular, Judd nevertheless shambled his way slowly into the kitchen this morning, gingerly rubbing a throbbing forehead with one hand

and smothering a yawn with the other. Opening the refrigerator door, he found Opal had packed him breakfast, lunch, and dinner – enough for two days.

Grabbing up the paper bag he knew held breakfast, Judd snatched his hat off the peg by the backdoor and made his way outside, crossing the yard to the tool shed, where he stored a Long Island brew of apple cider to wash away his aches and pains. Had it been a weekday, he would have downed a cup of coffee to wake himself, but the Tennessee Eastman didn't need his services this particular day. Judd lowered the tailgate of the '48 Dodge, making a seat there upon which to enjoy his breakfast outdoors.

If Opal and the children had been home, they would have eaten their breakfast together at the dinner table – something Judd took pleasure in. However, the three were off visiting her people in Ducktown, a place Judd knew well. It was where he had proposed marriage to Martin Hayes' oldest and prettiest daughter.

Opal – petite, dark-haired, brown-eyed, and a Baptist – had caught Judd's eye three years before that memorable day. She and he had courted one another ever since. When Judd finally asked her old man for permission to marry her, he knew the answer before he ever spoke to Martin Hayes. As expected, he was turned down quicker than water slides off a duck's back. Nevertheless, Judd had already purchased the ring at a pawnshop in Greeneville and had sprung the question while he and Opal were picking blackberries for preserves in the field just ahead of the Hayes' home place.

"I believe we'll make a good life together," he had said, "that is, if you'll have me, Doll. Marry me?"

Opal had looked up at him, those eyes of hers smiling, and set her basket on the ground. She then proceeded to wrap her arms around Judd, hugging him tighter and longer than anyone in his life had ever done. He lifted her into the air with one arm around the small of her back while still holding his bucket nearly full of ripe blackberries. She had accepted his offer before she ever even saw the ring.

Not long after, Frank Hall took them in his old farm truck to the courthouse in Jonesborough, Tennessee. Judd was twenty-four and Opal was seventeen when they wed. It was October 31, 1942 – Halloween day. Martin Hayes never forgave Judd Moore for this.

Fourteen years they had been married now. Judd shook his head in amazement, thinking how lucky he was to have such a good wife. He took up the cider jug from beside him, curling his left index finger through the handle, and brought it to his lips. The liquid burned going down. It always did of the morning. Moments later, a carefully prepared egg sandwich lay removed from the paper bag alongside three strips of bacon from a separate napkin. He thought again how good Opal was to him – even when she was not around.

Breakfast finished, Judd picked up after himself – folding the brown paper bag back over again for another time, then tossing the dirty napkin into a five-gallon bucket in the back of the truck, sealing the container so no trash would blow out while driving. Circling the tool shed, he made his way to the chicken coop laid out beneath the shade of a sprawling old Pecan tree. Tossing a few handfuls of seeds on the ground, Judd listened for the new chicks, hearing them before he ever saw them scurry out with their prideful mother hen. As he watched, he inwardly smiled at their young, inexpert attempts to scratch at the earth and peck up its riches.

Dawn's soft light had already given way to early morning. Looking up, Judd cast an eye beyond the chicken coop and pigpen, over his land, where the sweep of the side yard dipped into a small valley. The gardens there and all but the crowns of the two far hillsides still lie in cool shadow.

Across the valley, Judd spotted his favorite goat, an old white and gray patriarch. When he called out, "Hey Billy, Billy, Billy," the animal lifted its horned head, studied Judd Moore and stopped his chewing, then trotted down the hillside, around the fence line, and up the slope – halting ten feet from the only human being he trusted. They faced one another in mutual respect.

With a nod, Judd scooped out some feed, and then poured it into a pan for the Billy goat. He backed off and watched as the goat approached and went to work on the feed. Checking Billy's water supply, Judd grabbed up a pail and headed for the pump, filling the bucket without spilling a drop. As he topped off the goat's trough, Judd sang out, "Waterloo, how are you? I got a jug full and so have you." Then, tipping his hat to his four-legged friend, Judd rose up the cider jug from off the ground for mighty sip, while a Nanny goat and her two kids joined Billy.

There were many tasks to do this spring day – chop some wood for the coming winter, finish concreting the front porch – but getting drunk was the undeclared priority. So it was that Judd Moore spent this Saturday on up into the late afternoon. The cider jug was nearly drained of Ransom Bishop's special blend by the time Judd poured the first layer of concrete for the new porch, smoothed it out, and waited for it to dry. His hands were always busy.

"Busy hands are happy hands," he always told his children.

"Idle hands are the devil's playthings," his loving wife would usually add.

As afternoon eased on towards dusk, Judd grabbed up his axe and headed with a stagger for the woodpile to split the rest of the Hickory and Walnut he had hauled from Green Shed the weekend before. As he approached, the two piles of wood slowly merged duly into one. Laying out each piece, one after the other, on the circular chunk of Wild Oak he used for a chopping block, Judd split the round pieces with one downing of his axe. Then he took each of the halves and split them again – sometimes a third time – until he was perfectly satisfied with their size.

Once finished sizing up the hard wood, he began stacking the pieces at the side of the house, then covered the heap with a large sheet of construction plastic, and laid a cinder block on top at both ends. There was still a stack of softer pinewood to be reduced to kindling – easier work. As his axe rose and fell, Judd's mind wandered back over the years. He stopped a moment, turning up his cider jug to drain it of its last drops. Wiping his right hand across his mouth, he laughed aloud as he took up the axe and resumed chopping. A bright memory of his son's first awkward baby steps had drifted unexpectedly to mind.

Little Roger had taken three drunken steps forward, two to the right, and one back to the left, trying to steady himself before sitting back down in the front yard with a look of surprise. Judd recalled how Roger just sat there a moment, thinking things over it seemed. Then all at once, he put both hands on the ground to his front, pushed off, and stood again. With barely a wobble, the little guy had proceeded to walk straight over to Judd as he knelt watching. Judd remembered rising up quick, lifting his son into the air with both hands; Roger giggling, smiling, and spreading his arms out like a young bird spreading its wings

The memories washed away in a sudden flood of pain that flashed up Judd's arm. He looked down and, with oddly detached clarity, saw his severed left index finger lying upon the block amidst crimson-colored shavings.

"Hell fire and blazes – I done cut myself good!" he called out in shock.

Judd fumbled a handkerchief from his front pocket and wrapped it around his left hand, trying to staunch the flow of blood. Then he stumbled around to the front of his house and yelled out to a neighbor across the street, "Mr. Younts, you may not like me too well, but I'm bleeding pretty bad over here and could use your help." These were the first words Judd Moore recalled ever uttering to Oddie Younts. Nevertheless, his willing neighbor dropped what he was doing and ran quick to attend Judd's injury.

Mr. Younts removed the blood-soaked handkerchief, examined the wound, and said, "Let's get you to the clinic."

"I don't need no doctor. I'm about a quart low on oil but my engine is still purring," was Judd Moore's response.

Oddie Younts shook his head in disapproval, and then firmly added, "You are going to bleed to death if you do not go to a doctor." This was persuasion enough.

By the time they pulled into the clinic parking area, Judd was lightheaded and seeing double without the moonshine. His arm had gone numb from loss of blood. He looked to the driver side and saw a man he knew without knowing. "Thank you," he said. Oddie Younts smiled, "Anytime."

Inside the clinic, there was not much of a wait, but there was paperwork to fill out. Mr. Younts took the clipboard and pen from an attendant and began filling out the forms. He would ask Judd the questions and fill in the blanks accordingly.

- *Full name?*
- *Judd Moore.*
- *What is your middle name or initial?*
- *I never needed one. Don't reckon I have one.*

Oddie Younts filled in the address without having to ask, and then continued.

- *Birth date?*
- *October 13, 1918.*
- *Place of Employment? Where do you work?*
- *Tennessee Eastman.*
- *Sex?*
- *Thursday night... HEY - That's really none of your business.*
- *Never mind. I should have known that one.*
- *What are you sayin'?*

Oddie Younts grinned and told Judd what this particular question meant.

- *I knew that.*
- *Mind in the gutter, Judd?*
- *Most days.*

Sunday evening, Opal and the kids returned home. T. R., Opal's younger brother, dropped them off in the road to the front of the house. He tipped his hat to Judd Moore, who was working on the porch, then took off down the road.

Roger, now nearly ten years old, had brought home a sandy-colored mongrel puppy he'd fittingly named "King." Judd reached out with his right hand and took the dog by the back of the neck from his son's grip. The puppy did not make a single sound. He looked the pup over, and with a grunt of approval, pronounced, "He'll do," then added, "but he's your responsibility. You'll work to pay for his food or anything else he requires. And keep him away from my chickens and goats."

"I will."

Roger gathered King up into his arms, then caught sight of his father's bandaged left hand, "Wh-What happened to your hand, Daddy?"

"I lopped of my pointer finger while choppin' wood." The reply was delivered in a casual tone designed mostly to slip by Opal.

"You what?" Opal was not so easily sidestepped.

Judd kept his eyes on his work.

"I don't remember much. I was drunk."

"Of course you were drunk. You sure you weren't fightin'?"

Judd sighed, sat back on his heels, and looked Opal straight in the eye.

"I'm sure. Now let me be for a spell so I can finish this corner of the porch."

He resumed smoothing out the concrete.

Opal could see Judd was in no mood for further discussion, so began herding the kids around the side of the house towards the back door.

"Roger!" Judd called out after them, "C'mere for a second, would ya?"

Roger set King down and ran back to where his daddy stood. Judd removed a pocketknife from his overalls, opened the blade, and handed it pommel-first to his son. "What is today?" he asked.

"Sunday," Roger replied, adding, "May 29, 1955"

"Write that date here into this wet cement," Judd instructed.

Somewhat baffled, Roger carefully took the open blade and etched May 29, 1955 into the corner of the porch. Looking up at his dad, he offered him the knife back.

"It's yours," the old man said, "A boy ought to have a pocketknife. You just be careful with it this time. You hear?"

Roger wiped the blade with the front of his tee shirt, closed it carefully, using the side of his leg, then put the knife in his pocket. His pleasure in the gift was momentarily blunted by memory of losing the privilege of knife ownership a year ago. The cut had been an accident, but his sister would always carry the scar.

"Thanks," the boy said, kneeling down to pet his dog.

Judd looked at his son, perhaps guessing his thoughts. He cleared his throat.

"Don't be telling your momma this," Judd whispered," but I buried that finger about five inches below your marking in the porch." His son's smile was answer enough.

Suggested Listening: *Rye Whiskey by* Tex Ritter

Winesap

Compassion is the basis of all morality.

-Arthur Schopenhauer

A *story can be told a thousand different ways. Deciding whose side to tell is the trickiest part. I'll tell this one the way the Kingsport Times told it the day of the occurrence, then I will point out the shady areas at the end.*

It was sun up, yet overcast, and just after 8am.

"You ought not go in there," an inebriated fellow named Gus warned, "Buzz McClain is shootin' up the place."

Zeke Click turned immediately back to his Ford Coupe and retrieved a .38 snub-nosed revolver from the glove compartment. Then he cautiously opened the back entrance door and slid silently into the still darkness. His eyes focused almost instantly, but he already knew the way and could enter the establishment blindfolded.

"They had better be at least eight hundred in the till," a gruff voice was shouting, "Let's go J.C. Open it up!"

But J.C. Henry sat nervously upon a stool behind the bar and had never had a gun pointed in his face before. His shaky hands had lost all control when Buzz lowered the pistol and fired off two shots. One of the bullets struck the big toe of J.C. Henry's left foot. Despite the sudden pain, J.C. stood quickly and Buzz raised the gun and squeezed off another shot.

"God damn you Buzz. May He damn you to Hell."

The bullet pierced the closed tavern door behind him. J.C. Henry fled with a limp for his life as Buzz McClain rounded the bar and began removing bills from the register and stuffing them into a pillowcase. Clyde Lucas, another tavern employee, stepped away from the bar with his hands raised.

"You do it," Buzz shouted, tossing Clyde the sack.

Upon his exit J.C. Henry bumped into his boss Zeke Click who immediately muffled his cries with a hand clapped firmly over J.C. Henry's mouth.

"Shh," Zeke mouthed, "How many are there?"

He held up one finger and J.C. nodded "yes", then whispered, "Clyde, too."

When Zeke rounded the corner he was unnoticed still by the thief and he leveled his .38 and clearly demanded, "Put the weapon down, Mr. McClain."

Buzz McClain ignored the order and watched as Clyde removed the last stack of bills and stuffed them into the sack. He kept the pistol aimed at Clyde.

"Last chance, sir," Zeke commanded, "Put the weapon down and lift your hands into the air."

Like a top Buzz spun around smoothly, redirecting the pistol, but Zeke squeezed off a shot first. The bullet went clean through Buzz's chest, out his left shoulder, and grazed the right arm of Clyde Lucas. Buzz collapsed onto the sawdust floor and began cursing incoherently.

"You alright, Clyde," Zeke asked.

"I th-think so."

"I didn't want to have to do that Mr. McClain."

Zeke Click called the authorities stating, "I have just shot a man."

He not only rode along in the ambulance with Buzz McClain, the man who would have robbed his establishment Club 81, but he stuck around the hospital until Buzz was stabilized and even paid the hospital bill for him. Despite what the papers might have said, Zeke Click was an honorable man. Most who knew Zeke Click described him as a decent individual, well-mannered, and extremely generous.

And Buzz? Well – Buzz not only survived this altercation as I'll share later. He lived to be an old man – right up until just a few years ago. In his younger days he was shot a total of eight times: once by Zeke Click, once by Earn Manis with a shotgun, and six times by Ransom Bishop.

Buzz spent seventeen days in intensive care. He survived this meeting literally within an inch of his life; the bullet missed his heart by less than an inch. Because he had small children and a pregnant wife to support, Buzz had to return to cutting hair before he really had time to heal.

There are two sides to every story. I've heard this tale told every way one could think of. I've heard it told that there was a hit placed on Buzz McClain due to a real estate dispute. I've heard it told like the paper said. And I've heard it told from the standpoint that there was ill blood between both men. It was just a matter of time before such an event made the news.

It is imperative to point out that not everything made the news back then, not every murder or robbery got the authorities involved, and some individuals just turned up missing. A carpet might be rolled up and thrown out, buried, or even burned with unknown contents inside. Carpets could be replaced.

Suggested Listening: *You Win Again* by Jerry Lee Lewis

FISHIN

Challenges are gifts that force us to search for a new center of gravity. Don't fight them. Just find a different way to stand.
                                                        -Oprah Winfrey

Pastor Collins lifted up his Bible and announced, "I believe it would be the Christian thing to lay this dissension out onto the table."

One lady stands up on the left side of the congregation and declares, "I did not say it."

Another lady across on the right side of the

congregation stands up and says, "Oh yes you did."

All said – half of the church got up and walked out, including my Dad. It was Sunday. He'd rather be fishing with his friends, Eddie and Johnny Davenport. In his masterpiece novella *A River Runs Through It* Norman MacLean describes fishing as a spiritual experience with God. Some people from Northeast Tennessee agree with him.

When my Dad was still a little boy, he had a serious drug problem; He got drug to church on Sunday mornings.

What was said, I am told, was a downright shame. It was a comment uttered one time, then the comment was repeated and compounded through a Christian grapevine that wound in whispers all throughout each pew, finally reaching the ears of the large family of seven children it was uttered about.

It was "Why do all those children have patches on their pants?"

That family never attended church services there again.

Suggested Listening: *The Fishin' Hole* by Andy Griffith

Upstream

To keep the heart unwrinkled, to be hopeful, kindly, cheerful, reverent that is to triumph over old age.

-Amos Bronson Alcott

When Papaw drove past Springdale Baptist Church, long before he attended services there, he would always wave at whoever was standing outside. Usually everyone would acknowledge him, nod or wave back, but one time this old man ignored him and Papaw screeched his truck to a halt and wanted to know why that old man didn't speak to him.

Whenever we were going somewhere I would hang my arm out the side window of the passenger seat and casually wave at folks on their porches or cars passing by- often prompting people to wave back.

"Folks sure are friendly today," he'd say.

"Yep. What about that," I'd agree, proud to have assisted the mood.

Sometimes we would drive along Moreland Drive and out Pactolus to the bridge where nature was calling him. I had a bucket to catch minnows and crawdads. I'd spent what seemed like hours out in that creek catching whatever creatures I could locate. I caught a big Snapping Turtle one time and that sucker was mean. It could snap a stick in two with one lightning fast chomp.

Bottom line: my Papaw was a cut up. He was always playing pranks on people he liked. When he drove down McKinney Street and passed a group of kids he'd take his left index finger, the one that was halfway gone, and make it look like it was rammed all the way up a nostril. The neighborhood kids either thought he was crazy or just finger fishing for the elusive and often colorful Booger Trout.

When he stopped to pick Mamaw up from services at Springdale Baptist, he sat with his truck idling and Pastor Collins would usually come down and talk with him about whatever two friends talk about. Papaw thought a lot of Pastor Collins, a good and decent man – who cared about all God's creatures – even the notorious ones like the merciless Snapping Turtle and the mischievous Judd Moore

Suggested Listening: *A Month of Sundays* by Don Henley

Pecking Order

EDIBLE, adj. Good to eat, and wholesome to digest, as a worm to a toad, a toad to a snake, a snake to a pig, a pig to a man, and a man to a worm.

- Ambrose Bierce

Head Man and Hawg Man were well known killers – contract killers, who – through word of mouth and hard earned reputation, engaged in one murderous deed after the next all over Northeast Tennessee. These butchers, it was widely rumored, just might have been the most efficient under-the-table professionals east of the Mississippi River.

They traveled by truck – a 64 Dodge – with Stick Man, a crotchety cuss known to smoke three packs of Lucky Strike cigarettes a day. Head Man despised the odor of cigarette smoke - as did the Hawg Man. Both agreed there was a much sweeter aroma and flavor dispelled by a cigar blunt or a left-handed lucky.

Strategically- enroute to their next gig, Head and Hawg would play clever trickery upon poor Stick Man.

If poor Stick was positioned between Head and Hawg, it was imperative he keep his Lucky Strikes holstered in his front shirt pocket or else everyone in the cab would light up.

If Stick lit up, like synchronized swimmers at the Olympic Games, Head and Hawg each removed a smoke of choice, struck a match off the dash board and puffed their blunt or joint to a glowing life – making sure their partner Stick shared in their pleasure. Then they rolled their windows up all the way.

Drowning in fumes, "Damn it to hell," Stick scowled.

"You knew better," Hawg would remind him.

"Yep. You knew better," Judd reassured Stick Man.

If Stick was riding shotgun, he was terrible with a rifle, and always insisting on a cigarette, so his partners would instruct with great pressure he not only crack the window, but position his mouth near that one inch crack to keep any plumes from entering the vehicle. This was quite impossible on a rainy or snowy day and the winter season was the very best season for killing.

When the exchange was complete, the trio headed back to their Boss Man, Clay Rodefer. Quick as a wink, Stick Man would jump from the truck and seek out Mr. Rodefer to tell him of Head and Hawg's mischief.

Head Man once parked on the hill facing the Eastman Bridge and when Stick Man opened the door to jump out Head Man let his foot off the brake and let the vehicle roll back, causing the passenger door to swing back into Stick man, knocking him back into the road – just missing the back wheels. Stick Man cursed his cohorts and dusted off, then ran over to Mr. Rodefer to lodge another complaint.

"Uh huh... Uh huh," his receptive boss would nod, taking a slow sip of liquid from a mason jar before he encouraged Stick to "tough it up and wash up" for there was "still plenty of work to be done."

Mr. Rodefer, Head and Hawg Man would wait until Stick was out of sight, and then bust out laughing.

"Got him good, didn't you?"

"He was squirming like a Night Crawler getting the hook," Hawg advised.

"I'd liked to have seen it all boys."

Without direction – Head Man and Hawg Man went and washed up. Cleanliness was vital to their trade – as was a nearly painless death for their victims. These victims had squealed on their masters and it was time to silence them.

Hog killing took a team of highly skilled individuals.

The mastermind of the outfit was Clay Rodefer, a veteran of World War II who fought in *the Battle of the Bulge*, and is still a seasoned leader, and cunning prankster his self. It was Clay who first began calling me by my own nickname – *Auctioneer.*

Mark Rodefer, Clay's son, is Hawg Man. He earned this nickname because he not only knows every thing there is to know about killing, cleaning, and slaughtering a hog – but he can squeal exactly like a hog does if anyone ever asks him to. And we grandchildren took great delight in hearing his impression of a hog. Mark is a scoutmaster these days, teaching boys how to be virtuous and how to be crafty and survive anywhere. He should have his own reality show where they drop him off somewhere and he lives off the land. He'd have no problems sharing lessons to anyone willing to learn them

Bill Carr was called Stick Man because he was the one responsible for the initial stabbing of the animal. He would stick a blade into the swine's throat, severing the jugular. I think it is also because he stuck around – even though his co-workers were always giving him a difficult time. Bill passed away recently; lung cancer.

Judd Moore was called Head Man – not because he was in charge for he was definitely not – but because it was his job to take care of cutting the animal's head and around the face. He used a special butcher knife with a six inch curved blade to meticulously cut along the jowls then, with great skill, he inserted the blade between the skull and first vertebrae to sever the head from the spine. The head was then placed upon a cutting block and worked on in much greater detail. Aside from the burr of the ear, nothing was to be thrown away.

Suggested Listening: *King of the Road* by Roger Miller

TEXTURE

A person who chooses to die or to risk death demonstrates that there are values, principles, maxims, that are more valuable to him than is life itself. In short, he places his immortal self above his mortal self.

-Henry David Thoreau

When I was about five years old, if someone asked me what I wanted to be when I grew up, I gave them the most honest answer known to me at the time: a junk collector. Not like Fred Sanford from the show *Sanford and Son* but more like my Papaw Judd and his marvelous woodpiles and piles upon piles of building supplies and other odds and ends. He'd picked up much of this assortment by the side of the roads he traveled – back roads and highways. Most of the wood in his piles came from the Tennessee Eastman's discarded stock on Long Island. Locals called it *The Woodpile*. Roughnecks and Yuppies alike frequented *The Woodpile* in search of materials and Judd Moore made a daily visit part of his routine before and after he retired from the Eastman. After a visit to Mac's in the morning we would often make our way to *The Woodpile* to gather what we could among the scavengers.

Surveying the other vehicles and people at *The Woodpile*, he drove up slow. I made it a point to observe him peripherally as he watched the other people that were present ahead of us. If he shook his head to either side, I knew someone was there he didn't want there – someone who cherry-picked every good piece of timber out from underneath those who might really need it – only to try and sell it to them later. A scraggly man he called Hartsock was a man I knew my Papaw disliked. The cantankerous Hartsock would load up his truck with everything it would hold then continue to stack materials up against the fence next to his dirty white Ford where he left his son Hartsock Junior to watch until he returned with an empty truck-bed. I saw one confrontation between my Papaw and this man Hartsock and it was pretty intense – to say the least.

We'd been at the pile for a short time and Papaw had gathered a few pieces of two by four and some cinder blocks and placed them onto the bed of his truck. He then spied a large piece of dark walnut about a foot wide and twelve feet long. The looks of it reminded me of a pirate's plank. He snatched up one end and asked me to get the other, then we loaded it onto the truck and my Papaw continued his conversation with a friend of his named Dobbs.

"So how you been Judd?" Dobbs had asked him.

"Oh, can't complain – wouldn't do any good. Better than half, I guess. And you?"

Before Dobbs had a chance to answer Hartsock sped into the gravel parking lot laying on the horn and pointing at my Papaw's truck. Dobbs shook his head, "No trouble here Judd in front of your boy."

"I'm sick of this one Dobby, sick of him. *He's a snake in the grass,*" Papaw reasoned.

Before Dobbs could grab his shirtsleeve my Papaw had stepped away from him and planted his feet in front of Hartsock's dirty white Ford.

Hartsock laid on the truck horn and rolled down the driver side window. Letting off the horn, "At's my two by eight Moore! Put it back!" he yelled out. Judd Moore bent down and grabbed up a handful of sawdust, then stood back up.

"Make me."

I looked at my Papaw, and then glanced at Mr. Dobbs whose jaw had dropped and eyes had widened as he watched this unexpected showdown. Then I turned my attention to the white Ford – the engine now revving and the horn being blown again. Hartsock's son, a stocky built high school kid with rotten teeth and wearing a ball cap, walked over to the driver side door and stood there a moment mumbling to his enraged father. The shrill horn of the Ford suddenly subsided and the revving of the engine became a low purr. Hartsock's boy stepped quickly around the vehicle and got in. The scraggly driver waved his middle finger at us all, kicked his truck into reverse, and left in the same manner he had arrived.

Papaw Judd opened up his hand and the passing wind blew the sawdust away.

Suggested Listening: *TNT* by Hayseed Dixie

Cessation

It is time.

The captive audience
Surrounds the stage;
Patient prisoners
Without a cage.

It is time

To go back to the bottom.
Good-bye to Autumn
As the cool passing breeze
Sends children of trees

Marked by disease

In a flurry and hurry

To their inevitable ending
Gradually descending

Like lost searchers

Into unknown realms.
Winter's wrath overwhelms

American elms.

It is time

For immunity,
Equal opportunity,

Good-bye community.

Shall we go to the river –
Shed our skins with a shiver?

Frozen currents deliver

Us into the universal sleep –
With dreams so deep.

Let the willows weep.

It is time.

The captive audience
Surrounds the stage;

Patient prisoners
Without a cage.

It is time

To go back to the bottom.

Sourmash

You couldn't get hold of the things you'd done and turn them right again. Such a power might be given to the gods, but it was not given to women and men, and that was probably a good thing. Had it been otherwise, people would probably die of old age still trying to rewrite their teens.

- Stephen King

Judd Moore worked hard through the week operating heavy equipment (dump trucks, bulldozers, pans, cranes) for Tennessee Eastman Company. One project he was especially proud of was helping to reshape the Holston River. The river wound through Long Island much like a large snake, and every year, several times a year, it flooded the entire plant as well as the community there. So the *Powers that Be* decided to unbend its banks into a straight line. This was no ordinary task for the heavy equipment crew, and it was one my grandfather, when finished, counted as a very memorable achievement. He kept 8 x 10 black and white Kodak pictures of the undertaking, first with the Holston snake coiled around, then each process showing the progress made, until the completed result. To this day, it has remained unchanged.

"Cowden," Judd barked, "if I beat you to the lift, the drinks are on you tonight!"

"It's a race, then," his willing friend replied.

The mud-caked pans moved over the earth like elephants marching through the desert, a little faster than their usual languid pace. Judd shifted the machine down a gear, floored the juice, allowing him to pull ahead, and then shifted the machine back into high gear about seventy yards from their destination.

"Cecil," Cowden yelled out, "slow him down for me, would you?"

"Oh no," Cecil Hunt answered quickly from his truck, "I'll not be pissing Judd off on any Friday's end."

The lead elephant bellowed with laughter hearing this, removing his black cover, and raising it into the air in victory. Cowden threw his own hard hat into the cab's floorboard.

"Dammit," Cowden hollered, "I won't be buying you a drop tonight!"

"Whoa, Gal," Judd said, easing off the gas and applying the brake. As the rig came to a halt, he stepped off fast to get in front of the approaching machine. Cowden stopped the vehicle just inches away from Judd.

"Get down from there and say that again," Judd offered.

"You heard me, Moore. I ain't buying anyone a thing."

"I haven't beaten you yet, friend, but if you'll step

down from there I'll sure let you know what a real beatin' feels like."

Other men from the crew circled their vehicles around the growling dozer and the man in front of it. The engine shut off and the driver jumped down. There was silence, but for the whispers of the onlookers.

Hal Cowden stood around six feet three inches without his work boots on - six feet four and a half this day. He had always been, and was always known to be, a man of his word. He was a good worker, too, a *mountain of man* who stayed busy, did his share of the load, and was liked by most who knew him.

"Truth is, Judd, I'm a changed man. Hell, I mean – well - I don't rightly know what I mean, but I got saved, "Cowden admitted.

"Saved? Well then – have a drink on me, tonight, Hal," Judd said, "I've looked under nooks, crannies, and a few speckled panties and still ain't found the Lord myself. Where was He?" al Cowden extended his right hand, "I'm givin' up drinkin'." Judd took his friend's hand to shake it, and then punched Hal hard in the stomach with his left fist, knocking the wind out of him.

"You'll still buy me a drink," he doggedly reminded his co-worker.

Later on that evening at Club 81 Judd, Cecil, and the heavy equipment crew – including Hal Cowden – were sharing some potent moonshine brew out of a few blue mason jars. Judd removed a cigar from his shirt pocket, stuck it in his mouth, and lit it with a Zippo lighter he'd won playing poker. His hands fumbled but managed to unbutton his long-sleeve flannel shirt, remove it, and tossed it toward a nearby stool, but it landed on the sawdust floor.

"My friend Hal has found the Lord. We're

celebrating!" Judd stammered.

Hal Cowden was half drunk and feeling just as ornery as he arose from his seat – not to justify his actions, but to address his friend's simple remark.

"It's true ya'll. I don't rightly know what it means, but I got saved!"

Ransom Bishop from the table in the back of the room shouted, "You two shut the hell up. I'm trying to finish a damn hand of cards here and can't concentrate." The room went silent. Like pure reflex Judd Moore stepped swiftly but awkwardly towards the table then flipped it - cards, money and all into the air.

Hack Click, part owner of the place, eyed him closely, knowing full well what was about to take place. Ransom refused to make eye contact with Judd as Hack handled the situation.

"Sorry Judd, but that's it. No more booze – friend – and I mean it," Hack said flatly.

"I ain't your friend, Hack," Judd countered, sticking out his muscular chest like a fighting rooster and flexing his arms with a bit of a sway in his posture. His five feet eight inch frame was as solid and impressive as a marble statue of Hercules.

"How about you join us, Judd?" Ransom offered, "Hal, too. Let's celebrate."

Speechless, Judd felt his anger subsiding. He took a puff of the cigar, and then returned to Hal's side, lifting the flannel shirt from the floor. Ransom Bishop and company set the table back on all fours and gathered what had spilled to the floor while Judd put his shirt back on. Patting Judd on the back, "Maybe it's about time we quit this kind of livin'," Cowden offered.

"I reckon so," Judd responded.

Hal and Judd agreed to one last game of cards. The

mountain of a man Cowden and the chiseled Herculean Judd Moore joined the card table. Their actions this night were far from heroic, though. Truth is, Judd Moore was one helluva card player but once drunk he was as unlucky at cards as a woman taking a piss while standing. This particular round he lost a bit more than he had to give and was so upset he was fit to fight and dynamite on one poor fellow. A woman named Zola even busted a jar over Judd's head at Club 81, trying to get him off her boyfriend. He was knocked unconscious from the blow and may have suffered a concussion from the strike as well. The blood ran out his britches legs on both sides. Hal Cowden and Earl Medlin carried him out of the establishment and to his vehicle where they sat him in the driver's seat. He finally came to, punching the horn on the steering wheel.

"Are you alright to drive home, Judd?" Cecil asked him.

"Hell yes, I am fine."

And with that said he started the pickup and headed home. He was out of sight in no time at all and made the right up McKinney Street. After topping the hill, though, he judged the curve wrong and took out Mr. Spencer's mailbox, pole and all, without even noticing the post box embedded in the front grill of his truck.

Suggested Listening: *Sixteen Tons* by Tennessee Ernie Ford

Falling Back

Autumn is the bite of the harvest apple.

- Christina Petrowsky

From day one the old man hadn't liked me. Sure, he used to pet me every now and then behind the ears when I was little, but that was always the extent of any kindness he showed me. I watched him leave of the mornings and return in the evenings. I watched his ways. He was predictable and routine. Soon after I had grown much bigger, he would growl at me in the morning as he got into his truck to go to work. And, it was a different snarl when he returned home in the evening. I'm King – by the way. I am Roger's dog.

I think one of the reasons he might not have liked me is because I took up for Roger. One time, the old man chased Roger out into the yard with a switch, and I ran him back into the house and saved his son from a whipping. I am pretty large dog.

Another reason might be that some time ago I had chased down his prize rooster, the one he fought and made some money with, and kind of bit into the bird's neck a little too hard when I caught it. I did not kill the rooster, though. I probably would have if the old man had not hurled a big rock into my backside. I hated whenever *someone threw a rock at me. Things that ran from me deserved to be chased. I figured they had done something bad and thought they had gotten caught, like the old man when I ran him back into the house that time.*

When my father was only fourteen years of age, he had his first real glimpse of death when he lost one of his best friends to a drunken act. It was early one morning in the autumn of 1960.

Judd Moore had awakened just before the rooster crowed, except he was in a less familiar place than beside his loving wife in their bed. He awoke, stiff-necked, and sitting back in the seat of his truck and still drunk from a hard night of gambling. He had lost half his wages playing Poker, and then had beat up a man for looking at him the wrong way. Judd's knuckles were bloodied and still freshly hurt without any scabbing. The man's face had done quite a number on them. Judd smelled as if someone had poured a jar of moonshine over his head. Maybe someone had busted a container over his head, because it stung a bit. He reached back and felt the spot that hurt, finding a gash in the back of his head. Bringing his hand back to his front, he noticed the fresh blood on his fingers from the wound. His shirt was torn at the sleeve where someone had pulled him off the man he whipped. Opal had just gotten up to prepare breakfast but the children were still sleeping when Judd Moore stepped in through the back door and used the wall to stand as he looked smiling at his wife. Suddenly, he turned back toward the back door, opened it, and hollered out, "Shut up!"

Opal could hear King barking outside when her husband had opened the back door. Judd Moore, shaking his head in disapproval, closed the door, then – with a bit of a stagger – stepped into the kitchen toward his wife.

"Wash your bloody hands, Judd," she told him – with her own disapproving way.

The dog's barking became louder and Opal could hear it plainly now. Judd stepped swiftly to the back door, grabbed his loaded rifle that rested beside the pantry, then opened the door and stepped back outside. Opal moved quickly to the back door and saw her husband crossing the driveway toward the commotion. Then she ran into the children's room and lightly shook her sleeping son awake.

"Roger," she whispered – not wanting to wake Debbie, "King is out there botherin' your Daddy's goats again and your Daddy has gone outside with his gun. He's drunk, Roger."

Her words instantly woke her son from his dreaming.

Without even realizing we was moving, Roger, still in his underwear and barefoot, lifted out of his bed and ran out the front door and around the side of the house to the backyard. The morning dew chilled his feet as he walked over the gravel driveway. Then he stopped to find his father. He heard King barking, then saw two other dogs chasing his Dad's goats. King had befriended the other dogs over the past few years. One of the dogs was Dwight's dog Smokey. The other was a lop-eared stray hound that everyone threw scraps to and fittingly called "Scraps." Roger then saw his dad standing above the garden area on the hillside. He was aiming his gun at one of the dogs. But which one?

"King!" the boy yelled out, "King – get over here!"

The dog noticed the boy and stopped his chase.

The ring of gunshot deafened Roger's ears this morning and the bullet's destination pierced his own heart as he watched his dog fall over from the impact. He grabbed up a large chunk of gravel from the driveway and hurled it across the valley toward his father – who was already aiming his rifle at the two dogs retreating. The rock bounced off the ground in front of Judd Moore, then hit him in the kneecap. His gun fired again, but the bullet soared into the heavens because the rock had messed up his aim a great deal. Roger grabbed another chunk of gravel then ran down through to the garden area where King lay barely alive. The garden soil was muddy and squished between the boy's toes. This would have tickled any other day, but not this mad day.

Roger knelt down and wrapped his arms around his friend's neck.

"Don't die. Please don't die. I need you here, King," he pleaded as any life left his dog.

"I am sorry, boy. I am so sorry," Roger told his dead dog, looking up at his father whom was limping down the hillside toward him in the garden. Roger, angrier than Judd Moore had ever seen him, arose with the gravel chunk clutched tightly in his right hand.

"Put the rock down, son," his dad told him. Roger stood, facing his father, and did not drop his rock.

"Put the rock down!" his dad ordered.

Roger could smell the moonshine on his father from ten feet away. Judd could have threatened a whipping like none other before or could have apologized, but it would not have changed his son's mindset at that moment. As his father came closer, Roger reached back as if to throw the gravel chunk.

"I'm goin' in the house, son," Judd advised as he stepped around the invisible perimeter his son had formed.

Roger waited until his old man was some distance from him, then his anger came to a boil and he threw the rock at his father. It was as if it had sailed in slow motion through the morning air directly toward the back of his father's head. His old man toppled over to the ground and was motionless.

Silence.

Thinking he had killed his father, Roger ran back up the hill, across the driveway and toward the porch where his mother stood watching the whole affair.

"Daddy killed King, Momma," Roger said.

"I thought he might. That's why I woke you up, so you could get control of your dog and maybe your Daddy," she then continued, "Where is your Dad now?"

"He's laying down there on his belly above the garden. I think I killed him, Momma. I didn't mean to," he said.

"Let's be sure he's dead," Opal said, knowing her husband was tougher than her son may realize, as she took her son's hand, walking him back down to where his father lay. Noticing Roger was only in his underwear, she advised, "You'll catch a chill, son. Go into the house, put your robe on, then you can come back out here."

Her son turned reluctantly back toward the house. Opal went to her limp husband and nudged him in the ribs with her foot. He did not move. She knelt down and examined him. She noticed a gash in the back of his head and dried blood in his hair.

This was no fresh wound.

She lightly touched the gash with her hand, then noticed her husband twinge with pain. He soon came to and rolled over, looking up into the eyes of his loving wife.

"What have you done, Judd?" she asked him.

"Huh?" he answered

"Roger loved that dog, Judd, and you had to go and kill it," she said firmly.

Judd shook his head and said, "He was messing with my goats, Opal. I told that boy to...."

Opal interrupted him, "What is more important – the happiness of our son or those damn goats? Now get up and bury his dog for him."

Suggested Listening: *Old King* by Neil Young

Peeling Away

People like you and I, though mortal of course like everyone else, do not grow old no matter how long we live...We never cease to stand like curious children before the great mystery into which we were born.

- Albert Einstein

Every other weekend – we saw our Dad. He would pick us up in his maroon 1984 Ford F150 and take us back to the place we grew up – Kingsport. Songs came on the radio that I thought were written just for us. One song in particular seemed to be the most powerful to me at the time:

Missing You - John Waite

"Every time I think of you, I always catch my breath
And I'm still standing here, and you're miles away
And I'm wondering why you left
And there's a storm that's raging through my frozen heart tonight
I hear your name in certain circles, and it always makes me smile
I spend my time thinking about you, and it's almost driving me wild

*And there's a heart that's breaking down this long distance
line tonight
I ain't missing you at all since you've been gone away
I ain't missing you, no matter what I might say "*

Although I am certain Mr. Waite probably wrote the
song about a woman – it made me think about this
sudden shift my family was forced to cope with.   It
seemed this was a difficult time for almost everyone
involved.   I could see confusion within in my father's
eyes - even at a glance.   He was feeling a similar inner
torment – the kind that rips and tears with questions that
have no clear answers.   My brother, too, was dealing
with the divorce in his own way.   The *Moore Boys* needed
to get away from those questions – even if just for a little
while and our ringleader knew just how to cheer us up.
Without a word to confirm – Roger Moore eased the
truck off the highway onto a back road we'd never taken
before.   There was a sense of awe and wonderment when
the road became all ours.   The trees passing by the
moving vehicle seemed to welcome our arrival with
applause.   The unknown was beckoning us and we were
all ready to embrace it.

My Dad smiled and slowed the truck down, then
turned the wheel hard right onto a muddy dirt road
that led into the woods toward Bays Mountain.   We
sped toward the first large muddy puddle and Kevin
stared at me and grinned as my eyes got really big
and I grabbed onto the *Oh Hell* armrest and my body
tensed a little.

"Hold tight," my father laughed as the truck
accelerated.

He hit the pool at a good speed, sending water up
in a filthy spray at both sides of the truck.   I could

see the road through the front windshield when this happened but was more interested in the side views when the water was in full spray. The dirt road wound around the mountain for miles and miles. My father somehow already knew this. But my brother and I were just finding it out.

Suggested Listening: *Lost Highway* by Hank Williams, Sr.

Twilight Traffic

Traffic light control:
          where to stop,
               and when to go -
Whether to proceed
          with caution -
               or risk a heavy toll.
Are we not driven
          to our ends
    → like sheep into the fold → →
Sacrificed to society
          coats pitch dark -
               as black as coal?
We pause at intersections
          to find
             life is no open road
Offering every direction
          where to stop,
               and when to go.

Reservoir Dog

A hungry dog hunts best. A hungrier dog hunts even better.
- Norman R. Augustine

As recompense for murdering King, a dog my father reared from pup-hood into adolescence, Judd Moore tried to make up for his son's loss with a pure bred replacement. The replacement was a fully grown red Doberman Papaw won in a card came off Reservoir Road. He'd won the beast from a gentleman named Trick Wagner.

Trick had a famous distant cousin named Kinnie whom in 1925 gave the authorities a fit on Long Island, killing a few officers. Pete Dykes wrote a fine book about Kinnie Wagner told from the observant eyes of one Pug Potter. But that is another story; one Pete strikes far better than any match I could every light.

The Red Doberman was called Sid and he was one vicious S.O.B. When Judd drove the canine home he had to secure the giant dog with a logging chain in back of his pickup truck. Once home he had to keep the animal in front of him on the chain to keep from being bitten. Judd hammered a stake into the ground and kept the animal chained up to get used to his new home. Sid soon enough learned the boundary before him but he tested it every chance he could whenever someone came to feed him.

Roger would have nothing to do with that dog. Actually – Roger couldn't have if he tried. He told his friends, Hoyt and Dwight, "This dog is just like my Dad; he will bite you and he won't back up." He hated even the thought of King having a replacement – pure bred at that.

"He's the real deal, though - pedigree for sure," Dwight told him.

"Pure breed dogs are dumber than mongrels, Dwight," Roger informed him, "Surely you know this."

"How so?"

"Well – pure breeds have a tendency to be inbred by the breeders – for one."

"Like folks in Erwin," Hoyt joked.

Roger and Dwight laughed.

"Also," Roger continued, "Mutts pick up the strengths of that melting pot of bloodlines."

"That's a load of crap," Dwight said.

"Better dump your load then," Hoyt chimed, "cause I'll be a monkey's uncle we're about to see the theory tested."

The Way family just across the street had a brave little male Bulldog/Dachshund mix named Filo who weighed maybe twenty-five pounds. But Filo thought he was bigger than he was. He had been a buddy to King and still a friend to Smokey, Dwight's dog. Filo learned the big Red Doberman's perimeter the first day he ventured into the Moore yard to piss on some trees and flowers now that his buddy King had been slain and buried down the hillside from the hog-pen.

Filo nonchalantly covered nearly every piece of bush, shrub, and tree as the boys watched. The little dog turned his attention to Sid – who had stirred up the most awful commotion, with his hair spiked up on his back and up his neck like a deranged cat, he began to growl really low and circle the perimeter. The Red Doberman was irate – venting and slobbering all over with each pounding of his front legs onto the grass by the time brave little Filo walked up directly toward him. Sid was as *fit to fight* as a Grizzly female protecting her cubs. Filo walked up slowly to the fuming animal, bared his pretty white teeth, and then pivoted his body. With a hike of the leg Filo had urinated onto the red and brown face and legs of the chained beast. Then he kicked his hind legs back one at a time and sent dirt and grass onto Sid. Sid was left to stew like an unattended crock pot already boiling onto the stove. The boys watched the events play out like they would have an episode of Rin Tin Tin.

"I told you," Roger announced, "And it is 'O' - fficial."

Sid's temper was tried fully within a mere week and that reservoir dog upturned the stake, dragging logging chain and all, and bolted across the street seizing the Way's dog by the throat in a death lock before Opal Moore could *bat an eyelash*. Sid wasted no time establishing that Filo may have won a minuet pissing contest but he was not by any means the stuff he thought he was.

American Humorist Henry Wheeler Shaw in the 1800's said, "A puppy plays with every pup he meets, but an old dog has few associates." The same is so for us humans if you think about it.

Suggested Listening: *Waterloo* by Stonewall Jackson

Morning Glory

It is the mark of an educated mind to be able to entertain a
thought without accepting it.

--Aristotle

Dad rented an apartment after he and my Mom separated, and he still worked a forty-hour week at Tennessee Eastman with all the overtime he could handle. Since Dad still had to report to work some weekends, it afforded us time with the ultimate babysitters on God's green earth – our grandparents, Opal and Judd Moore.

Mac's Crack was a reference I heard many times throughout my childhood from my Papaw. "If you're goin' to go to Mac's Crack with me, let's go," he'd say as he stood in the doorway of the guest bedroom, then he'd turn into the darkness and head into the kitchen for his hat. I would slide out of bed, gather up my clothes and drowsily get dressed with the light still out, throw on a ball cap and my shoes and walk towards the back of the house to the bathroom. I would take a washrag and wet it with cold water, then wipe the sleep from my eyes, dry off my face and head out the back door toward the tool shed/garage. His truck was already idling and warm. He was always in the driver's seat listening to country music playing low on the radio - older songs like The *Battle of New Orleans*, *Ring of Fire*, and *My Buckets Got a Hole in It*. These were the songs he could choose to sing along to word for word or change the lyrics into a humorous and often vulgar spin that kept us grandchildren laughing. One song I remember well went like this:

> *Tomcat on the fencepost.*
> *Pussycat on the ground.*
> *Tomcat may jump on the pussycat's ass*
> *And they both went round and round.*

"S - T - O - P," he would chuckle as he eased on the brake, bringing the apple red dodge to a halt at the bottom of the hill coming off McKinney street., "Stop. It says so on the sign."

I'd smile and wait for the next sign. Although he couldn't read, I always knew in my mind he was a smarter than most anyone I'd ever know. I did believe he could read any road sign.

"D - I - P... Dip. Him? Oh, me? Why yes, I'll have a pinch," reaching into his coat pocket to produce a tin of Skoal, then giving a sigh – only to talk himself out of any taste until after breakfast.

The Golden Arches of my Papaw's favorite hangout

illuminated the skyline in the still darkened sky of a 6am morning. We'd often pull in a few minutes before opening time and he'd sing along to whatever song was found on the radio or he'd just make one up. Sometimes he would lean forward and stare off through the windshield as if in a trance. Then he'd suddenly realize his departure and turn his attention back toward his passenger – or in some cases – passengers. It wasn't uncommon at all back then to have three or four of us grandchildren piled into the cab alongside Papaw driving. Somehow he never had trouble shifting gears.

When the restaurant did open we were rarely the first ones in the door. Businessmen with deadlines or tee times often hurried ahead, ordered their 35 cent coffee to go, and then stealthily snatch a 25 cent newspaper under their jacket on the way out. There were usually four or five newspapers placed in the racks for customers inside use so it was important to go ahead and claim one. If my Papaw didn't set one on our table, I took great pride in collecting one for him.

I settled down in the bench like seat to dissect my Hotcakes and sausage, and then fooled with poking a straw through an aluminum orange juice lid, fumbling around until my breakfast was fully prepared. Then I engaged in the precise ritual of eating one thing at a time. My Papaw unwrapped his sausage biscuit then removed the patty and placed it upon a napkin. He took another napkin and lightly patted the top of the meat to get any excess grease from it, then wadded the napkins with one hand and placed the meat back on the biscuit with the other. Next he took the lid from his piping hot coffee and poured in creamer and a pack of sugar, stirring it with a miniature straw and returning the lid to the styrofoam cup.

Before my Papaw took his first bite of biscuit or

sip of coffee we were usually joined by people he knew – either from Eastman, Springdale, or Mac's Crack. John was a middle-aged man who played high school football with my Dad. Jimmy was another frequent addition. He had white hair and always wore work clothes and a smile. There was another man my Papaw just called Preacher. To this day I have no idea whether he was a minister or not, though I do remember hearing a few dirty jokes from him that my Mamaw would have taken offense to, but not us no good heathens.

Suggested Listening: *Common Man* by John Conlee

PIECES

Spend the afternoon. You can't take it with you.
                                        -Annie Dillard

During the warm months in the afternoon, the entire lot of us would insist on riding in the truck bed. It's difficult to explain but there is an infinite sense of freedom and even a majestic feeling in the Spring and Summertime with the sun shining down and the world passing by at fifty-five miles an hour.

If Mamaw came along, she would always ride in the cab with my Papaw and sometimes whichever kid was misbehaving, too. For lunch my Mamaw preferred Long John Silvers, which stood right beside my Papaw's preference of Mac's Crack. I'd usually eat with Papaw because the only thing I liked at Long John's was hushpuppies.

Upon noticing my Papaw enter the restaurant a cashier would usually yell to the back, "Juddburger!" We grandkids were quite amazed at my Papaw having a cheeseburger named after him. I never ordered one myself but I knew what was on it: bun, meat, mustard. The only thing missing from Mac's trademark cheeseburger was ketchup and onions. We would sit down with our food and I would be nearly finished by the time my Papaw was done patting the grease out of his burger onto a napkin.

I can't think of a single time I saw Judd Moore in a hurry. I recall, as a kid, feeling like Papaw's pace was ten times slower than my own. It must have been years and years of experience that taught him prudence because even now, after all these years, I find myself making careless mistakes and getting in a hurry to do everyday things that call for patience and not the anxiousness that seems to follow me. Whether I am eating a meal or driving across town, I can hardly wait to be finished.

Although many might argue this with me, Judd Moore was punctual in all things as far as I know and he never appeared to be rushed.

Down in the Papaw patch as a young kid, maybe six years old, I was picking beans along side my Dad, Mom, brother and my Papaw Judd. I had covered the bottom of a brown paper grocery bag and was probably complaining or daydreaming and my Papaw had just filled his bag.

"Give me a poke," Papaw said.

I shrugged, stood up, and stepped over to him and poked him in the ribs with my index finger.

"No, silly – a real poke – a bag," he disclosed in frustration.

I didn't know what a poke was and am glad the first time I'd heard it wasn't in high school from some girl I had a crush on. I would have probably asked if she wanted kissed some first.

Suggested Listening: *Remember When* by Alan Jackson

The Core

The seed of God is in us. Given an intelligent and hard-working farmer, it will thrive and grow up to God, whose seed it is; and accordingly its fruits will be God-nature. Pear seeds grow into pear trees, nut seeds into nut trees, and God-seed into God.

-Meister Eckhart

When Judd stepped out the backdoor and down the steps the sun had not yet risen and the sky was still a midnight blue. The rain was drizzling steadily with a slight chilly breeze constant upon his face. The wind wasn't strong enough to blow the old gray Stetson from his head. And the Stetson was cover enough to keep him from getting very wet at all.

"No sunshine today at all, I'll bet," he thought, "No

worries. I can still do what I've planned whether Mother Nature is in a foul mood or not."

I often thought back on the wisdom my Papaw imparted to me. Most of the time he was merely making an observation out loud - like when he dissected an apple. Why did he extract the seeds before eating the fruit? I assumed it was because the pips were hard and difficult to chew. But he gave the answer anytime he caught me watching.

"Poison," he would say.

How did a man who'd had two days of schooling know that all apple seeds contain Prunasin, a cyanogenic glycoside, which is a chemical that becomes a poison when it is digested because it releases cyanide? Well, I doubt he knew all those big words, but he knew the basic truth of the matter.

Other tidbits and knowledge he passed along involved work and education – both of which he considered important attributes to possess an understanding of. His education was self-taught and learned from his own experiences. No doubt he had many teachers; Sergeant Yates from his basic training in the military. It was Yates who taught a twenty-four year old Judd Moore how to sign his name. Yates was also one of his first genuine friends; Mother Nature who everyday offers lessons to those willing to pay attention. Judd paid close attention as often as his sobriety allowed. She had awakened him once – her voice booming down on him as the rain nearly drowned him in a sewer ditch on Long Island; His loving wife Opal taught him how to give love and how to receive it; L.C. Collins taught him through the years that the devil resided everywhere - in a jar of moonshine, in his own actions, in the hearts of others

– and the only way to deny the devil was to recognize him and start building walls to keep *Old Slew Foot* away; His children Roger and Debbie taught him much about himself also.

Suggested Listening: *A Country Boy Can Survive* by Hank Williams, Jr.

Humble Pie

"Defeat is not the worst of failures. Not to have tried is the true failure."

George E. Woodberry

At age ten I used to flex my little muscles like a bodybuilder, even posing in the mirror. My older brother Kevin was always a little bigger than me and much stronger. He posed in the mirror, too. Perhaps he knew his muscles looked more impressive than mine because he even practiced his smile in front of the mirror, too. When we arm-wrestled back then Kevin always won. One time I thought I had the advantage but he was just toying around with me – just before he raised my arm slightly and slammed my hand to the table

"Not so hard on the table!" my Mamaw hollered from the living room.

Papaw stepped through into the kitchen and tapped my brother on his right arm.

"Blood vein on a rat's leg," Papaw said, smiling as he rolled up a shirtsleeve just above his forearm.

"Wanna give this old man a try, big boy?" he asked.

The challenge had been made. I got up out of the seat

and let my Papaw sit down. He had a mischievous grin on his face as he placed his right elbow on the table and offered up his hand. Kevin seemed a bit reluctant at first then positioned his own elbow on the kitchen table and locked hands with his challenger.

"Hold on, son," Papaw presented, "you're clutchin' all wrong."

Not expecting the teaching lesson – I paid close attention as Papaw showed my brother the way arm-wrestling was supposed to be performed. Instead of locking hands palm-to-palm in a backward handshake, the thumb knuckles crossed one another, and the hands gripped at a different angle.

"Jason, if you'll start us off," Papaw instructed with a wink in my direction.

I placed my hand on top of their clenched hands.

"Ready... set," I began, noticing Kevin's intense eye contact with a faint hint of fear. Papaw was not a delicate man, so I know my brother was not afraid of hurting him.

"Hold on," Kevin stopped "we do it the other way if you beat me. Okay?"

"Either way," Papaw offered him.

"Ready... Set," I began again, "Go!"

I watched with great delight as Papaw – without strain – taught my brother a lesson in humility... twice. Before my brother could recover from getting beat I challenged him to Papaw's way of arm-wrestling. He humbly declined.

I'd heard stories about the days when my Papaw was a bit younger and known for his inhuman strength. Though he lost money playing poker and pool, he'd never lost money arm-wrestling. He was one person few would dare tangle with, but many would accidentally provoke.

Witnesses at the S&M shop at Eastman have advised me that Judd Moore many times lifted a five hundred pound "Headache ball" into the air so it could be attached to a crane's chain or cable.

Some guys at the Rodefer's Garage on South Eastman Rd. witnessed a prank played upon my grandfather in a testing of his strength.

There were three anvils at Rodefer's garage of varying size and weight. This certain blacksmith's anvil at Clay's establishment that weighed around one hundred fifty pounds, though, was one my Papaw boasted he could grab by its horn with either hand and raise it up to shoulder level. Bill Click stepped to the anvil and grabbed it with both hands and strained to lift it a few inches. He let it drop back onto the table.

"Too awkward! Hell no, Judd. You can't lift it – not with one hand," he warned.

J.D. "Peezer" Halkleroad nodded in agreement with Bill.

"He-he-h-h-he's r-r-right, J-Ju-Judd."

Judd Moore stood by the anvil and informed the men, "I'll lift it and you doubters can pay me a buck each when I'm done."

"And if you fail?" Clay Rodefer asked him.

"Two bucks each," Judd offered, "but I won't."

Confident and calm, he pulled a stump of cigar from his shirt pocket and placed it in his mouth. John Spencer produced a lighter to light the cigar but Judd told him, "Not yet."

Scroochie, a co-worker of Judd's in the early 1940's was present as well. He and Papaw helped clear the road that leads up to Bay's Mountain City Park. He is the only one that refused to wager against Judd, knowing full well what he was capable of.

The usual crowd had gathered, including Ransom

Bishop and Harry "Hal" Cowden. Silence ensued as Judd clapped his hands, then rubbed them together. Facing the anvil, he knelt down onto one knee and reached out with his right hand to grab the horn of the anvil. Then he picked it up from the table and stood with it steady in front of him at shoulder level. Judd held it out for about twenty seconds, then lowered it back down to its usual resting spot.

"You just weren't holdin' your mouth right, Bill," Judd said as he switched the cigar stump from the right side of his mouth to his left.

Then he knelt down again and reached out with his left hand and grabbed the horn of the anvil again. Same result.

Nodding to John, he leaned forward and his friend blazed his cigar to life.

"Damn him. Done it before," Ransom muttered as he dug out a silver dollar and placed it on the table beside the iron anvil.

All told – Judd made seven dollars that day, which was a lot of money in 1951.

He performed this feat anytime he stopped off at the garage on his way home from work or mischief. And he usually only made a few dollars doing it because no one was ignorant enough to wager against him twice. One time, though, Papaw's friends got him good. On Tuesday, October 13th of 1970 those friends and some of the heavy-equipment crew greeted Judd Moore late in the evening. Clay's teenage son Mark stepped forward and shook Judd's hand.

"Dad told me you used to be really strong," the boy said, "and I'll bet you ten dollars you can't raise that anvil up like these guys claim you can."

"That's a serious wager, son. But if you'd like to lose some money to me – I'm all for that."

"I'll bet against you, too, Judd. You aren't the muscular

man you used to be," Clay doubted, aggravating Judd's pride.

"Hawg's piss," Judd boasted.

"He's got a point," Hal Cowden agreed, "You've gone soft in your middle age."

Judd was steaming at the words – so mad he stepped through the crowd and to the anvil directly, reached out and took it by the horn, then was surprised by its weight. He strained to lift it even an inch. His arm shook, then his body.

"God bless," he shouted, not giving up. Another few inches. *Thunk*. He released it.

The crowd began to clap as Bill Cleek and Cecil Hunt produced the hundred fifty pound anvil that Judd usually grappled with. They carried it out like a cat they might pitch in the creek and placed it beside what looked like its twin.

"This is your baby here Judd. That other is a bit heavier," Clay informed.

"How much heavier?" Judd asked.

"At least seventy –five pounds."

"I'll get it up next time," he chuckled. He removed two five-dollar bills from his wallet and handed them to the boy.

"You got the goldmine, son. I got the shaft."

"Happy birthday," Mark said, "you keep it."

"Damn. Well, it is my birthday. I knew I was forgettin' something."

Scroochie came forward with a birthday cake my Mamaw had made.

"Fifty-three candles are all lit here Judd. You'd better blow'em out quick before all this icing melts off," he instructed.

Suggested Listening: *Woke Up This Mornin'* by Alabama 3

Forbidden Fruit

"You are free to eat from any of the trees of the garden except the tree of knowledge of good and bad. From that tree you shall not eat; the moment you eat from it you are surely doomed to die."

- God

It has never failed – in studying any culture's offering of chasms and byways in history, folklore, and mythology and all the way up to the present – I've surmised anything humankind is prohibited from doing – they will always do anyway; sometimes just for the sake of breaking the rule. Lawmakers have to know this. No fences. No walls. True freedom is being able to experience whatever life has to offer – without arbitrary restriction. I can understand why some laws would be of importance, whether they are God's, Mother Nature's, or Mankind's. Man kind? Now that is two words that do not belong together.

The original story of Snow White is about her disobedience. She is made by her guardian to pick a white rose each day in a certain garden, and is told not to speak to anyone she meets. But as she is blossoming into womanhood a prince happens upon her in the garden and visits her secretly as each day passes. When she begins to lose her innocence the roses begin to change in color at first to pink and finally a bright crimson red. There is no way to hide her disobedience from her guardian, who attempts to separate her and her lover. This is where the apple comes into the mix.

After the titan Prometheus stole fire from the gods and gave it to mankind, man was able to forge tools, cook his food, and civilize himself. This sent Zeus into a rage because now humans could become more like the gods. The end result is the creation of the first mortal woman, Pandora, whom is told never to open a certain box. This is a story most people are familiar with and a prime example of disobedience.

When the president does it, that's means it is not illegal.
-Richard M. Nixon

A certain plant my Papaw Judd called "Coontail" may have had a worse reputation than even he did. But the plant's reputation wasn't always a bad one. In fact, during the 1600's farmers were ordered by the government to grow it. And in the 1700's because of a shortage of the plant - one could be incarcerated for not growing it. By 1850 there were more than 8,000 plantations growing it in America. Coontail is a very useful plant that can be used to make paper, clothing, rope, food, and much more. Contrary to anything the Federal Drug Administration will ever admit it also has medicinal value.

But during the early 1900's it was discovered Coontail was being used as a recreational drug and thus began its inevitable outlawing. Propaganda appeared in every newspaper, serving to degrade the plant. Fear-tactics – including themes of violence and racism must have been at their peak during this storied period of American history. We can blame Harry J. Anslinger for what came next in the newspapers. Examples:

1. *"There are 100,000 total marijuana smokers in the US, and most are Negroes, Hispanics, Filipinos, and entertainers. Their Satanic music, jazz, and swing, result from Coontail use. This Coontail causes white women to seek sexual relations with Negroes, entertainers, and any others."*

Can you imagine if this was printed in our own "Politically Correct" day and age? Is this what old-timers refer to as the Good Ole Days?"

2. *"… the primary reason to outlaw Marijuana is its effect on the degenerate races."*

Degenerate races? Webster's Dictionary definition of the word degenerate:noun: a person whose behavior deviates from what is acceptable especially in sexual behavior

Fans of racial categories up through the present day cannot approach this old world in a color blind way. Why should it matter if someone is of African, Oriental, Caucasian, Hispanic, Asian or Native American descent? Or whatever the heritage? Tell me why. I'd love to hear it. I'd love hear what parents are implanting into their children's brains about race, religion, and sex. All over this tired old world we humans are breeding and feeding hatred against one another. We are like a thousand little plastic Army men of every color and are shuffled onto the battlefield of life. And we have to ban together to either survive or we will surely self destruct.

3. *"Marijuana is an addictive drug which produces in its users insanity, criminality, and death."*

If this were true, then all the world's politicians are smoking left-handed cigarettes.

4. *"Reefer makes darkies think they're as good as white men."*

Truth be told – solid gold – we are all in this together and none of us is better than the other. Even the Green Man has been outcast, though.

5. *"Marijuana leads to pacifism and communist brainwashing."*

What is wrong with pacifism unless provoked? Scholars of history will agree that we are all brainwashed through secondary school. Is democratic brainwashing any better?

6. *"You smoke a joint and you're likely to kill your brother."*

I guess everyone who fought in the Civil War was smoking big fat doobies.

7. *"Marijuana is the most violence-causing drug in the history of mankind."*

Leaping Leprechauns Batman! Look at our world today! We should be smelling Jamaican Tobacco at every turn.

"Come. Let me show you my shop, mon."

This fit all to well the corrupt politicians' unseen agenda, protecting the corporate profits of the cotton and lumber industry and ensuring the typical right wing bullshit we are still dealing with today. On August 2, 1937 – Coontail a.k.a. Marijuana was made illegal at the federal level to sell, grow, and definitely smoke. By this time Judd Moore was a grown man whom enjoyed a jug of illegal liquor and whatever else the government might prohibit the public from using.

There are two modes of establishing our reputation: to be praised by honest men, and to be abused by rogues. It is best, however, to secure the former, because it will invariably be accompanied by the latter.

-- Charles Caleb Colton

Papaw grew Marijuana upon one of his friend's encouragement. He, his friend, and my Dad were the only ones that knew. He planted some seed behind his rickety garage. Those seeds sprouted and wouldn't stop growing. It flourished and the stalk became thicker than a goalpost. We grandchildren always thought it was a tree. In fact, I would use the giant stalk to climb up onto the rooftop of the garage and hide from my brother and cousins when we played War or Hide-and-Seek. If Papaw was outside working in the yard, I'd sometimes catch him watching with a grin on his face and shaking his head. Like Mona Lisa he, too, had a secret.

I experimented with marijuana a time or two. And I didn't like it, and I didn't inhale.

- William Jefferson Clinton

Ironically, the highest Coontail ever got me just might be on top of Papaw's garage.

With the flourishing success of the first plant it was determined he could do well growing a slew of hemp mixed in with a fairly good sized crop of corn. The stalks of both plants typically grew about the same height and no one would be too suspicious of a sixty year old man taking good care of his garden... no one but his wife Opal. She frequented the garden to pick tomatoes or beans and grew suspicious of all the weeds mixed in with the corn. Upon pulling up the stalks of hemp she played innocent with her husband and told him she had rooted up all the weeds from the garden and tossed them on the burn pile - a pile she made sure was already ablaze so no recovery effort could take place. Although this internally sent Judd Moore into a fit, he pretended to be grateful and decided it best to keep the *weed* from the garden after all. He found a good spot way back in the woods - well off the beaten path and profited some with the risk.

When Judd Moore retired from the Tennessee Eastman in 1976, the paper read, "Sullivan County native Judd Moore has a son, Roger, with TEC. Mr. Moore spends some of his time gardening around his home at 1829 McKinney St. The retiree is married to Opal Hayes Moore and the couple have a daughter, Debbie Barrett and two grandchildren, in addition to their son. Mr. Moore has made a home in the local area for 33 years and served with the U.S. Army Infantry."

I thought it comical they didn't bother pointing out what crops he was growing.

Suggested Listening: *(The) Most Unoriginal Sin* by Willie Nelson

PULP

The enemy is anybody who's going to get you killed, no matter which side he's on.

-Joseph Heller

I t was a troubled time for the working class. Although the Noble Experiment, Prohibition, was finally overturned in 1933 under Roosevelt's careful watch, many states still outlawed the buying, selling, and definitely drinking of alcoholic beverages. Tennessee was no exception. The state that pretty much paved the way for the Temperance Movement in the late 1800's was still no friend to what many conservatives had labeled "the Devil in a Bottle". Tennessee had been dry since 1909. Sullivan County was dry. And the city of Kingsport was a desert as well. This led a handful of fine folks to make their own brew either for personal consumption or immediate profit.

On Long Island in Kingsport there was Preston Sutherland who made a famous Bramble Mash Wine.

Bramble Mash Wine

1 gallon raspberries
1 gallon blackberries
1 gallon water
1 pound sugar
1 thin strip of muslin
1 five gallon stone crock/jug
10 one quart mason jars w/lids

He bruised the berries with his hands then let them stand overnight. Then he discarded the pulp, straining the blend, and mixing the liquid, water, and sugar. It was poured into the jug for fermentation and the thin muslin was placed over the top of the vessel. He knew when the mix had stopped "working" when the bubbles no longer appeared on the surface. Because fermentation times always varied with each batch, old Sutherland checked his blend religiously – twice a day. When satisfied that fermenting was complete, he then poured the wine into mason jars and stored them in the cool of the springhouse in his backyard. He generally made three to four batches a week but never more or less than his recipe called for. He sometimes traded his brew for dry goods or services but mostly made his living selling the wine for two dollars a quart from his truck-bed on weekends. That was big money in the 30's and 40's.

His temper, though, would be his undoing. Barney McNew, another Long Islander who enjoyed a stiff drink, had finagled some Bramble Mash from Preston, promising payment on his next payday. Barney was drunk more than he was sober. He ran up credit without paying regular and it was only a matter of time before he was cut off. After abusing Preston's trust for a spell, however, old Sutherland finally refused him wine without settling the debt.

"You selfish turd," McNew shouted, "I said I'll pay you next week!"

"Next week, month, year," Sutherland cut him off, "you'll pay what you owe me before I grant you another drop!"

Preston Sutherland was fuming by this time but McNew was equally upset. "Go away Barney!"

"Not without a taste."

Preston Sutherland shoved Barney backward into the street. Barney McNew's face got red and then he drew a switchblade knife from his pants, released the blade, and waved it menacingly, threatening to attack. He lunged forward, gesturing for Preston Sutherland to step away from the wine. Preston stepped away from the truck bed but produced a 22 pistol and aimed it at McNew.

"Touch it and you'll taste something far different," he explained.

Barney McNew persisted and was promptly shot in the side of the head. He was dead before he could know what hit him. Preston Sutherland was arrested a few hours later. He served some jail time but was released eventually. It is uncertain whether he made any Bramble Mash Wine or violated his probation after his release. I am told he worked as a half-ass carpenter for many years, though he didn't have a permit. He was killed in an untimely car wreck on Long Island.

Suggested Listening: *Drinkin' Wine* by Granville "Stick" McGhee, *Something's Gone Wrong At Home/Poor Boy From Home/When I Was Drinkin' by Sonny* Terry and Brownie McGhee

Aftertaste

Accountability in friendship is the equivalent of love without strategy.

Anita Brookner

Though silent the majority of his sober years, Judd spoke loudly though his actions - often defiant and stubborn - sometimes so damn ill-tempered that his own wife and children feared him. I never really did, though, except the time he chased me around the house after I broke a branch off one of his trees.

"Ease up, Judd," my Mamaw had called after him, "don't want you havin' another spell with that heart of yours."

He stopped abruptly and yelled out at me, "Sooner or later I'll get you! There's a storm a comin'."

And like some wrath from the gods it began to sprinkle just after he went into the house to have dinner. Thunder followed with the wind like some unwanted aftertaste. I shivered outside – trying not to cry, both afraid and miserable for what seemed like an hour or more before he came back onto the front porch, folded his arms, and looked a bit perturbed.

"Jason," he started, "You can come in now. You have my word. I won't whip you anymore. I know you didn't mean to hurt that tree."

His word was golden.

Suggested Listening: *Dueling Banjos* by Roy Clark

STAINED

Roger and Hoyt laid out of church one Sunday morning. It was pretty easy to do. They just never reported to their Sunday School class. Hoyt had two chicken eggs and he handed one to Roger.

"Here you go, old buddy," Hoyt declared, "we are gonna have a testing of strength."

"Whatever do you mean?" Roger asked.

"Well, Mr. Salyer tells me that no one has disproved his theory that an egg cannot be crushed by hands that hold it from both ends and push in toward the center."

"He gave them to you?"

"Kind of, I took them from Maxine, his old red hen. They're just laid too."

"C'mon -then let's see if we can prove him wrong."

Hoyt demonstrated the technique Mr. Art Salyer had showed him but his attempts were futile. The egg was unbreakable.

"Daggum it," Hoyt confirmed," he's right."

Roger tried with as much strength as he could manage with his egg, and he was much bigger than Hoyt, but found the egg's shell too hard to crack.

"Try it the other way," Hoyt told him, knowing the

result would prove different.

He did and the egg busted all over Roger's new shirt. After discovering the soiled shirt – Opal knew her son had laid out of church services and been up to no good.

Suggested Listening: *If I Were Clever* by Tammi Rhoton

Tree of Knowledge

Did perpetual happiness in the Garden of Eden maybe get so boring that eating the apple was justified?

- Chuck Palahniak

My Mamaw Opal was always a God-fearing woman and probably the closest person to a saint I'll ever know. It was with her that I first attended church services. We always walked the half a mile to Springdale Baptist Church where L.C. Collins was the minister. When I was very young, I got to stay in the nursery downstairs with the other children where we got to play games and hear stories like Noah and the Ark and Jonah and the Whale. Once my brother was old enough to stay upstairs with Mamaw it made it all right for me as well. I remember attending Pastor Collin's sermon the first time as a child. I sat on one side of my Mamaw and Kevin sat on her other side. Services began with the choir singing a few hymns then the director instructing everyone to stand and sing along. The lyrics in the hymnal were laid out like a puzzle - so confusing that I couldn't sing along because I couldn't keep up. The only thing I could halfway do right was stand up and pretend to sing along. My mind spun with questions the whole time.

I didn't really understand much about God, Jesus Christ, and the Bible at that age – just that the preacher shouted a lot and held a handkerchief in one hand to wipe any spittle off his mouth and chin. People ahead in the other pews got into what the pastor was saying. "Amen," they would shout or "Praise the Lord!" Pastor Collins was able to preach from his own experience when he spoke against drinking and gambling. He'd grown up in the Highland area where he and other children wore knives on their belts for protection. He'd seen a lot of sin or "Backsliding" as he called it. Like many young people at the time – he'd seen more violence and lawlessness than he should have. But growing up hard made him develop a tolerance and patience that he was able to cultivate into a noble profession. I'm not talking about his employment with the Tennessee Valley Authority at the John Sevier Steam Plant, but his founding of Springdale Mission in 1946.

His firsthand knowledge of sin helped him win many souls to his cause.

"There is something dead up the creek," he accused, "and you... *you* are not being honest with yourself or God." I sat there wondering what I'd done wrong. I wondered if my brother knew and might tell on me. I felt the preacher was speaking directly to me. Trying to ignore his words, I lowered my head in shame and decided I'd rather be with my Papaw Judd – wherever he was that morning.

I believe I had a bit of a drug problem also – getting drug to church like my Dad did. But Pastor Collins had a presence and energy and he could laugh and cry all at the same time when he "got happy". He was quite a man and an integral part of Judd Moore's redemption.

My Dad met a Buddhist in Vietnam and the man shared this with him:

A man prayed: O God, let me hear you.
The thunder roared.
But he didn't hear.
O God, let me see you.
A rose blossomed right in front of him.
But he didn't see.
O God, let me feel you.
And he brushed away a butterfly that landed on his hand.

Suggested Listening: *That's My Job* by Conway Twitty

MARKETS

So many of our dreams at first seem impossible, then they seem improbable, and then, when we summon the will, they soon become inevitable.

Christopher Reeve

My Papaw didn't attend church services until after a thirteen rounder with the reaper in the early 1980's. Though the reaper was due a rematch, I determined to make the best of the time we'd been granted. Otherwise, I would have never gotten to know the man. And he wouldn't have gotten to know me.

He went to flea markets instead of church. I started going with him on Sunday mornings and found the experience just as spiritual. This is where he taught me to haggle. He believed in never paying full price for something he wanted – only for something he needed. Haggling is an art form that both of my Papaw's taught me. What little time I've spent with my Papaw James Carter, my Mother's father, I learned that comic books were a thing of value. Before the introduction of comic books, though, I surmised I could collect knives, like my Papaw Judd did. Judd Moore had a very good collection of rare knives he'd acquired by trading and haggling with people at the flea markets. He was what we southerners like to call a *Horse Trader*. He finagled and negotiated a fair price each time – or did not settle the deal - not at all. James Carter was the same way. He'd walk away, but sometimes get called back *to square the deal*.

As I write this now – my daughter is nine years old and she is picking up the art form, too. I hope she continues to cultivate this craft and is some day passing how to haggle down to her own kids – my grandchildren.

Suggested Listening: *I Love* by Tom T. Hall

SPROUT

Both read the Bible day and night, but thou read black where I read white.

- William Blake

Opal Moore is a "headhunter". Everyone knows it. Anyone who's glanced through the family albums suspects it is true, but most aren't brave enough to ask for a confirmation. Once and future in-laws who become outlaws - through separation or divorce - have their heads summarily removed from group pictures. . If she has to remove the torso along with the head to get them fully out of the photograph, she does that, too. However, she keeps the heads. They are usually placed toward the back of the album on their own separate page with all the other heads of former in-laws

Definitely - at a glance - it looks very similar to an album cover by the Beatles titled, "Sgt. Pepper's Lonely Hearts Club Band." Generally speaking, my grandparents stayed on good terms with most outlaws - with the exception of just a handful of no goods who'd chosen to sever any ties with them. Debbie's first husband Danny Barrett was one of the first to be decapitated. My mother - yes - would ultimately have her head cut off, as did my Dad's first wife. It's funny because I am happily divorced as well and my daughter Bethany has been known to ask in an innocent whisper "Is that where Mommy's head was?"

Suggested Listening: *A Few Questions* by Clay Walker, *Good Hearted Woman* by Willie, Waylon, and the Boys

SINGLE DIGIT

(For Bethany)
She hums a carefree melody
-    when walking through wintertime
Instead of in the spring.
Nothing much to do
-    when the snow is melting - my
Girl loves to skate and sing.
Laughter and innocence
-    are the songs she shares
Eased by the moments passing us by.

Daughter, my dear,
-    you're growing up -
-    the *apple* of my eye.
I wonder now where you will go
-    the things you'll do and see,
Growing up is never easy
-    as the fruits fall from the tree.
In the chorus of the morning bliss
-    a brand new day will begin.
Tomorrow is an afterthought
-    when you're nine and turning *ten*.

Suggested Listening: *Free Fallin'* by Tom Petty

Springing Forward

Don't ever take a fence down until you know why it was put up.
Robert Frost

It was the middle of June in 1962. School had just let out for the summer. Roger and his three friends – Hoyt, Dwight, and Jerry - were already bored of the summer heat. Everyone who knew the boys knew they had a tendency to get into trouble. In fact, Hoyt's mother had just grounded him because he had helped blow a neighbor's mailbox to smithereens with an M80 firecracker. However, when his mother and father left for work each morning, he knew they had no way of knowing what he was up to unless someone saw him and told his parents or one of his siblings ratted him out. So, for the next two weeks he had to make sure that if he did anything, he would not get caught.

Hoyt persuaded his friends into meeting up over at Glen Alpine in Sullivan gardens for a game or two of basketball, his favorite sport.

The boys could have played at Springdale Baptist had it been a few months prior, but the elders of the church decided to take down the church's basketball goal because some of the neighborhood kids had been heard cussing during some games played a few times.

So far this summer, the temperature had reached at least eighty degrees each day, but the morning they were to play basketball a constant and unforgiving wind began to blow as the boys rode their bicycles a few miles down the road. The rising sun in front of the boys was soon covered by dark clouds and dawn began to look more like nighttime. The rumble of thunder came soon after. Then lightning could be seen in the distance. Suddenly a steady drizzle of cold rain fell on the boys followed by a torrential downpour.

"We can't play out in the rain when it's storming," Roger shouted to his friends.

"I reckon not," Hoyt agreed, "might get electrocuted."

The thunder boomed like a bombs blast all around the boys.

"Well," Dwight informed quickly, "we need to decide what we're doing 'cause we can get shocked just riding around in this mess."

They decided it best to take off for their high school because it was just ahead of them another half a mile. Roger, Hoyt, and Dwight rode at top speed and arrived at the front double doors of the school first. The doors were covered by an awning and kept the rain from drenching them further. Hoyt looked back towards the street but didn't see Jerry until a flash of lightning revealed his silhouetted figure just peddling his bike at a normal pace toward the school.

"Let's go Jerry," Hoyt yelled out to him.

"No sense in hurrying boys," Jerry answered loudly, "we're already wet!"

Because Mother Nature's wrath wasn't letting up the boys decided they would need to find a way to get into the school, but the front doors were locked tight. Jerry told the boys he thought he could get them in through one of the windows in the shop area. He advised, "Wait here. I'll be back in a flash." And then he stepped out into the downpour and disappeared around one corner of the building.

"Do you think Old Weaver's working this time of day?" Roger asked.

"I doubt there's anything to clean up while school is out, silly," Dwight answered him.

Old Weaver was the school custodian. He was what many kids called scraggly, toothless, and lacking in personal hygiene. It was rumored he had a criminal past and that his living quarters was somewhere in the basement of the school.

The doors behind the boys soon swung open and Jerry proudly ushered his friends inside. The thunder crackled long but was muffled by the door swinging shut behind the boys. The empty hallway was dimmer than the boys were used to while school was in session. There was silence without the usual sounds of several teenagers trouncing about. It was also a bit eerie with an unsettling feeling at first for the boys.

"Boo!" Hoyt yelled suddenly.

"Stop it," Roger said to him, then punched him hard in the arm.

"At least we're out of the rain," Dwight told them as he flicked the light-switch to find that the power must be out in the school. They slowly made their way back into the gymnasium where they agreed they could play a game of basketball. Luckily, they found a ball setting in the corner beside the bleachers.

"You're on my team, Hoyt," Roger informed him – passing the ball over to him.

"Fine by me," Jerry said nonchalantly, "Dwight and I will slaughter you guys."

After one close game to twenty-one the boys decided to take a break and huddled around the water fountain. Upset by their loss, Jerry grabbed a quick drink – and without a word headed back onto the ball court. He sat on the bleachers and pulled a cigarette from his back pocket. Luckily it wasn't wet. He lit it and took a slow draw, then leaned back on the bleachers and closed his eyes.

"Hey," Hoyt whispered, noticing Jerry lying back, "where'd that slacker get cigarettes?"

The three boys decided to play a prank on their daydreaming friend.

From out of nowhere Hoyt ran crazily into the gym carrying a fire extinguisher. Without warning he aimed the device at Jerry and sprayed him in the face, covering him with a white foamy powder.

"Uh, Jerry," Hoyt reminded him, "There's no smoking in the school."

"There's no trespassing either," Old Weaver's voice at the other end of the gym boomed.

Hoyt froze. He stood speechless. Jerry couldn't see to get up – still choking from the sudden prank. Footsteps approached and then all at once Roger clapped his hand on Hoyt's shoulder.

"Gotcha good, didn't I?" Roger asked

"I – I think I swallowed my cigarette." Jerry announced.

Dwight Conklin was laughing so hard he had to sit down in the gym floor to keep from falling over.

Suggested listening: *Old Friends* by Ray Price, Roger Miller, and Willie Nelson

Fruition

This existence of ours is as transient as Autumn clouds. To watch the birth and death of beings is like looking at the movements of a dance. A lifetime is a flash of lightning in the sky. Rushing by, like a torrent down a steep mountain.

- Buddha

When I was almost six years old, there was a very bad winter here in Kingsport, Tennessee. There was a lot of snow on the ground – so much that our Christmas break from school began a week early and ended a week late. This was wonderful for my brother Kevin and I and our cousins – because we were all able to devote more time to sleigh-riding and snowball fights than any of us were able to before then. Our parents still had to work, though, so someone had to watch over us kids. That someone, it turned out, would be my grandparents. They would never refuse to tell a story to us children. Mamaw kept several small children's books within an old cigar box.

When Jeff and Tammy were little, before my brother and I were a part of the equation, my Papaw used to sit them on his lap and open up a Little Golden Book. He would make up the most marvelous tales about the Pokey Little Puppy each time they asked to hear a story. His stories were never the same, but were always just as enjoyable as the real thing… if not better.

I am not sure how my Grandparents managed to accommodate or put up with five children all at once. But Opal and Judd both came from large farming families. Maybe that is the difference. We were known as the Bloomin' Wild Bunch to our parents and grandparents when the five of us ever got together all at once. This Christmas holiday would be different than any other we had ever known, though – not because of the fun we had, but for the single event that took place.

All of us kids had been playing in the snow to the side of the house, riding our plastic sleds down the hillside into the garden area. I walked back onto the porch and stamped the snow of my feet because I had to go back into the house to use the bathroom. When I stepped in through the front door, I noticed my Papaw Judd was on the phone an obviously a bit *choked up*. This was one of the only times I ever saw him use the phone and it was the only time I ever saw him upset to the point of nearly crying.

"I would appreciate if you would do this for me," he had said as he hung up the phone.

I walked on toward the bathroom but stopped when I came to my Mamaw who stood in the kitchen.

"What's wrong with Papaw?" I asked her.

She looked at me in a sad way herself and said, "Ask me again in a few hours." This puzzled me. It was rare for her not to just answer any questions I would ask of her. I went on and did my business in the bathroom, then ended up back outside to play – without thinking about my Papaw crying again.

I had been outside playing again for maybe fifteen minutes when my father pulled into the driveway with a sad look on his face. He stepped from the vehicle with his rifle, then walked into the backyard without acknowledging us children playing.

"What is Dad doing here?" my brother had said.

My cousin David quickly answered, "Roger had his rifle. He is probably going hunting for turkey so we can all eat some for Christmas."

Nope, that's not it," Jeff instructed, "He's come to shoot Pepper."

"Why would he shoot Pepper," I asked, "she's a good dog. She's never bit anybody I know."

"She's been sick for some time," Jeff pointed out, "she's as old as the five of us combined."

"That's like 100 dog years," Tammy said.

"Well, why isn't Papaw shootin' her? She's his dog," Kevin countered.

"Because Pepper is his dog he can't bring himself to squeeze the trigger," Jeff said.

"I don't understand," I said, and then a shot rang out. We all heard it, and it was followed by a dog's yelp. We were all very sad.

My Mamaw later told me more about the events of that day. My Papaw had taken Pepper, who had been crippled by cancer, to the veterinarian a few days before – and it was suggested that she be put to sleep. My Papaw's heart was broken, but he did not want to pay twelve dollars to have the doctor do it for him. So, he determined that he would dig her grave beside the doghouse and use a bullet to put her to sleep. The day after he left the veterinarian he spent the day petting Pepper and talking to her, telling her what he had planned to do. And he told her he would miss her when the spade first broke the hard frozen earth to form her grave. My Mamaw said he was silent the entire day and he was heartbroken.

When the hole was dug, he went back inside for his loaded rifle, then reluctantly made his way back to where Pepper lay suffering. Snow began to fall as he mustered the strength to aim the rifle where he knew the animal's heart would be, but he could not pull the trigger. He set the rifle against the dog house and knelt down to hold his suffering friend. My Mamaw had walked to them outside and asked him to come on into the house for supper. "I can't do it," he had said. "But it has to be done, Judd," she advised, "you know she is hurting, so pay the twelve dollars and let them do it for you." Some time in between that moment and his phone call to my father, he had made the decision to ask his son for help and the good Lord had decided to send a heavy snow to the area.

As I have become older and heard this story a time or two, as well as, the story about my Papaw – in a drunken act - killing King, my father's dog, I have come to realize a big difference in the two men I respect. My Papaw, I believe, was sorry he had killed his son's dog – but he never officially apologized. He did bury my Dad's dog, though. King was greatly missed. Dad always spoke of that dog as if he was truly his best friend. My Dad's mercy shot for Pepper was just that: Mercy. There was no motive – other than to put Judd Moore's suffering canine out of its misery. There should be no shame in a good deed.

Suggested Listening: *God Only Cries For the Living* by Diamond Rio

The Savage Garden

He who has injured thee was either stronger or weaker than thee. If weaker, spare him; if stronger, spare thyself.
- *Shakespeare*

When two dogs are left to fight it is usually to the death. In the animal kingdom some things have to be final. It was Eisenhower, I believe, who said *"a whipped dog will seek revenge."* In February of 1952 – not even five months after Zeke Click had caught Buzz McClain robbing his tavern, shot him, paid his hospital bill, and saw to his recovery – Buzz sought retribution.

The Cleek/Click Family Album describes Zeke as "neat, well-dressed, and a handsome man. He had several automobiles that were serviced at Copas' Esso. He preferred the V8 Ford Coupes. Most figured he used the automobile to transport whiskey…" It was told to me by various individuals that Zeke was a selfless and generous character. If he bought a newspaper and a cup of coffee for ten cents, he still tipped the waitress five dollars. That was a weekly paycheck for most folks. Zeke was shot and killed by Buzz McClain at his Long Island cabstand while he was playing cards with Ransom

Bishop. Nine shots were fired. Seven of them connected. Four were in the arm and three in the chest. Zeke was unarmed.

Buzz McClain's own mother told *Kingsport Times News* "The wrong man was killed".

Before there was a "Meals on Wheels" or a "Goodwill Industries" there was the Cleek Brothers. They made sure the poor, sick, and elderly of Long Island and Weber City had coal supplied for their furnaces for the winter. Groceries were purchased for the needy or credits paid in full at the store for some people. They also employed some fine folks, too, whom normally couldn't gain rightful employment elsewhere because of something shady in their past. Compassion and Tolerance, two virtues a politician will speak on and make promises about but not follow through with executing, were two virtues the Cleek Brothers excelled in practicing. The loss of Zeke Click/Cleek was a sore one for the community.

Buzz had his reasons, I am told. He believed he had been shot in the back those few months earlier at the tavern gun battle – based on the information the doctor had given him. Buzz was incarcerated up until the trial, but never had to serve a day afterward. Perhaps this is why after Buzz McClain shot Zeke Click he stated, "that's a shame."

Suggested Listening: *The Dance* by Garth Brooks

THUNK

I don't measure a man's success by how high he climbs but how high he bounces when he hits bottom.

-General George S. Patton

The first time ever breaking a bone I was lucky to come away from the accident with my life. I was eleven years old and summer was almost over. My brother Kevin, my cousin David, and I were spending the week at Mamaw and Papaw Moore's house. We had a way of always finding something to build or create from the various resources in Judd Moore's woodpile and tool collection. We had determined this particular week to build a fine tree-house. Supplies were to be gathered once a good location had been found. We'd found a hemp rope about twenty-five feet long rolled up and hanging in the tool shed as well as a small hatchet and surmised we'd need them for our scouting efforts. So David slung the rope over a shoulder and I grabbed up the hatchet. My brother Kevin, with a pencil nestled just above his right ear carried a clipboard and paper

We knew the trees in the main yard were off limits. Bottom line – Judd Moore coddled the various trees he'd planted. To build a tree house on any of his trees was pure vandalism. The pecan tree in the back yard was ideal but it was a no go. We headed down the fence line and up the hill toward the forest. A towering hemlock just across the barbed wire fence caught my eye

"What about that one?" I questioned.

"It's too close," David said.

"Too close to what?" I asked.

"The fence line, dumb-ass," David informed me.

Whack! My brother had smacked him in the back of the head.

"No one calls Jason a dumb-ass unless it's me," Kevin interjected, "Besides, look at the large branch protruding from it. It might be perfect."

"Perfect for what," I asked.

"A rope swing, dumb-ass," Kevin shrugged, "But let's keep looking."

"A rope swing would be cool," David acknowledged, thinking more on the subject "Screw the tree house for now. Let's get that rope over that branch you've spied. Jason, ole' boy, you're a freakin' genius."

I went from being a dumb-ass to a genius in a span of ten seconds. I wasn't the genius. It was my big brother Kevin's idea and insight. He was the engineer of the project. The tree did have potential and David was known for his skill in climbing trees. He was graceful and strong like an orangutan, fearless and agile like a gibbon, and his temper was like a silverback gorilla fixing to charge, too (Not to mention – his aerodynamic haircut would one day propel him into being one of the fastest white sprinters in the whole state of Tennessee.). At any rate – David ducked under the fence-line, gathered the hemp rope and started up the tree *quicker than three shakes of a sheep's tail.*

High in the rafters of the hemlock and out onto the branch, David balanced out like he was on a high wire, then bent low and grabbed a spot with both hands dropping his legs down, dangling for a second, and then he swung his legs up and wrapped them around the branch like an Army Ranger might negotiate a cable. Like an upside-down inchworm he moved out further with my brother navigating, "Just a bit more. There. Perfect."

Once the rope was secure David held it in both hands, wrapping one ankle around the rope, then he lowered himself hand under hand gradually down closer to the steep bank where Kevin and I were standing.

Before David could touch the ground with his feet my brother asked him, "Is that tree strong enough for a tree-house?"

"Good thinking, Kev," David exclaimed, then instead of coming the rest of the way down, he began to ascend back up that hemp rope hand over hand with the greatest of ease.

It was determined shortly thereafter that we'd settled on the perfect location for our tree-house. We began to gather other materials. Nothing was off limits as far as supplies went. Papaw was usually quite generous with the scrap wood he'd acquired over the years. Plus, he was gone that day, working for Stanley Hall and putting up hay, out around Hall's crossroads. So he wasn't there to persuade us otherwise.

It wasn't that I was the test dummy. Really, it wasn't. It was more that Kevin and David began to count the tree-house as the priority and they were busy up in the rafters of that tree finalizing the design for a fine tree-house.

"I'm gonna test this rope swing out boys," I told them.

Kevin looked down at me and waved an okay.

Grabbing up the rope, I stepped back then scanned

over the steep bank and was not afraid. Then David yelled down at me, "Here Jason. Wear these gloves." One hit me in the head and the other landed just in front of me. I picked up the goatskin gloves and put them on. They were a little loose, but I didn't think twice about it. I leaned back.

Here goes nothing.

Well, it was something alright. This was the very first day of my life I didn't feel invincible. I wish I could say I remember it well, but I don't. All I know is that I swung out and I went out as far and as high as the rope would take me – and even farther once the gloves had slid off.

Apparently, I was *pale as a ghost* after crashing to the ground in a face plant and tumbling down the rest of the bank into a briar patch. And Kevin had leapt out of the rafters of that tree and was checking on me almost before I had settled to a halt. David was *red as a beet*, I am told, when he hurdled the barbed wire fence and took off *like a dart* to fetch my Mamaw Moore.

"Stay with me," Kevin kept saying, "Don't go to sleep."

How did he know I was falling asleep? Was it instinct? Was there something within him advising him to keep me conscious?

"Talk to me little brother," he'd repeated again and again.

Then I began to speak – once the wind that had been knocked from me had been replaced with fresh air. Apparently I had given Kevin quite a farewell speech before Mamaw had ducked under the fence and began assisting with my recovery effort.

Can you wiggle your toes?
Y-Yes.
How about your fingers? Can you move your fingers?
No... wait... I can't move my hands. I think my hands are broken.
How many fingers am I holding up?
I can't see anything. I can't open my eyes.

Because my Mamaw Moore never learned to drive a car she didn't have a driver's license, so I had to wait on my Dad and his wife Barbara to arrive. But I believe Dad drove as fast as Kevin had leapt from that tree because - lickety split – I was lying in the backseat with my head on Barbara's lap and she was asking me questions, keeping me awake.

We had to sit in the waiting room a very long time. Apparently some racecar driver that came in after I did had to be seen first so he could be cleared and get back to the track to finish driving around in circles for money. I'd like to run circles around him while plucking the eyelashes off of whatever crew chief bastard had those strings pulled to get that driver back on that damn track, keeping me waiting in extreme pain and death-thrown trauma in that room full of miserable strangers who'd taken a number like everyone else.

After over two hours of waiting, it was discovered I had broken both my wrists, suffered my first concussion, and had to have my left eyelid sewn back on. The doctor hammered my bones back into place and then I was outfitted in a cast around each wrist and had to wear an eye-patch over my left eye for about two weeks.

Would you believe I was interviewed on two

separate occasions by some obese member of the hospital staff about how this accident happened? Two different times I was asked a series of similar questions about whether or not my Dad had beaten me up and I'd tried to fight back. My Dad has never been a violent person. If anyone deserved a beating, though, it was that race team and every racecar team out there that expects common people, especially a child, to take a backseat to a fractured nose.

When my Papaw, now sixty-seven years old, returned home and my Mamaw broke the news to him, he shook his head, swearing under his breath.

"I told'em. I told'em to stay off those trees. They'll get killed."

He immediately went to the Hemlock and ascended like a ghost up into its rafters, removed the twenty-five foot hemp rope, then threw the rest of the supplies down to Kevin and David – who would assist him in returning the tools to their rightful places. He looked out to where I'd fell, focused on the briar patch, then climbed back down the tree. Without a word to my cousin or brother, Judd Moore walked down the bank and stopped abruptly near the bottom.

Damn gloves.

Suggested Listening: *Dang Me* by Roger Miller

Shavings

You take a fraction of reality and expand on it. It's very seldom totally at odds with the facts. It's shaving a piece of reality off.
- Frank Snepp

One November morning of 1991 Judd awoke like always – never any alarm clock – never his wife waking him - just an internal clock ringing inside his own mind or heart telling him it was time to get up. Smothering a yawn, he dressed himself, and made his way slowly through the house into the bathroom, then closed his eyes and flicked on the light. Standing by the sink, he opened one eye to the lighted room and then the other. He smiled then turned on the hot water of the sink, waited for it to get warm, then plugged the drain and let the water fill up halfway before shutting it off. Judd squirted a dollop of shaving cream into his hand then applied it upward onto his face in circular motions. He shaved *downward, the way his whiskers would grow if he let them, in long even strokes. He pulled his skin taut before each stroke applying a firm yet light pressure. Rinsing the razor after every two strokes to keep it from clogging with hair, he thought about a lesson he once gave his son in shaving and a lesson his wife had given him that same day.*

The morning after a hard night of drinking in 1958 Judd Moore stirred in a chair in the living room as the sunlight streamed warmly in through the window and onto his face. A dog was barking loudly somewhere outside. He took in the smell and sound of bacon cooking from the kitchen. His empty stomach would not be denied.

"It's Saturday or Sunday," he thought, *"Thank the good Lord I am off."*

His head throbbed something awful and Judd aimed to drink that pain away, after breakfast of course. Judd stood and stretched, shaking each arm after reaching them toward the ceiling. Covering a yawn, he moseyed into the kitchen where his wife and daughter were.

"I love you, doll," Judd announced.

"Good then," Opal answered him smiling, "Wash up. I've made you something special."

"What is it?"

"You'll just have to wait and see."

"Good morning, princess," Judd said to Debbie. "A fine morning, Daddy," Debbie smiled, careful not to look at her father. Judd took note she seemed preoccupied with setting the table.

Judd stepped lightly toward the bathroom. The door was closed.

"Somebody in there?" he asked.

No answer. He knocked three times on the door then opened it and peeked in.

"Just a minute," a voice cried. But it was too late.

Judd had already witnessed Roger undertaking something that needed direction. Roger had shaving cream laid on thick all over his face. He looked like Santa Claus with a huge white beard.

"Hold on, son. You're going at it all wrong."

"I can do it, Daddy," Roger said, hoping to deter him.

"A father ought to show his son how to shave. Now step over and we'll do this together."

First thing of the morning since he was on his own, Judd Moore always shaved his face. This morning would be no exception. Roger stepped aside.

"All right then," Judd instructed and turned on the hot water, "First we have to get some warm water in this sink. We have to plug the hole and let it fill up about halfway."

He looked his son in the eye as he explained each step to him. He took up a towel and wiped the shaving cream from Roger's face. Judd cupped some warm water and patted it onto his face.

"You do the same," he told Roger.

His son doused the warm water onto his little face.

"Peach fuzz, little man," Judd offered as he touched the thin blond hair on the side of Roger's face. "It'll stay peach fuzz for a while if you want to change your mind, son."

"No, Daddy," Roger had already determined, "I believe I'm ready."

"All right. There's no going back then."

Judd then glanced in the mirror and felt a bit shocked. He did a double take and then a triple. Something obviously was not right. He looked closely into the mirror at his reflection. Something was definitely missing. He cupped more water in his hands then splashed it all over his face. Was he dreaming or was he the victim of some prank?

In ancient times a boy was considered a man when he had grown his beard. To my knowledge my Papaw Judd Moore never had a beard. I remember him always having a smooth shaven face. I know for a fact he was forced into manhood well before most and he only had about two days worth of schooling before he was made to quit so he could work on the farm.

Many months earlier – before the shaving lesson – Judd Moore had took the notion to grow him a fine moustache. He still shaved his face every morning – just not his upper lip. His wife Opal detested the stubble and pleaded with him to shave it off. She even threatened not kiss him until it was gone.

"You'll shave it off, Judd," she told him, "or they'll be no lovin' for you anytime soon."

"I'll n'er do such a thing," he vowed.

Her insistence upon the stubbles' removal was futile. He was proud of that moustache and planned on keeping it. It grew like an unrestrained fruit on his upper lip until finally it was thick and virile and curled at the ends in what seemed like no time at all. He fancied it like a woman fancies a diamond ring. Opal's pledge was kept. At times she became downright standoffish if he attempted to hug or kiss her.

My Daddy Roger was around thirteen years old then and still remembers rousing late at night to use the toilet. A lamp was lit in the living room. He could hear his father snoring like a mower starting then stalling over and over. Roger crept into the room slowly, careful not to wake his father. Roger's shadow passing along the wall startled his mother, though – instead who shushed him before he could speak. Opal held a straight razor in her right hand and dipped it into the washbasin. Then she waved her son to leave the room. For some reason nature wasn't calling anymore. Roger walked on into the bathroom anyway with his mind in a hurricane of scattered thoughts.

"*She wouldn't,*" he kept thinking, "*no way she would.*"

But she did. She only shaved off one side, though, of Judd's fine moustache and had left the rest for her husband to finish.

Though my Papaw had vowed to never shave off his thick moustache, he broke that vow. He was more humiliated than mad as he showed his son how to shave off the hair where it is long and thick. For the bushy half of the moustache that remained he first used scissors to cut it down some, explaining to his son the reason for trimming it first. Unwillingly losing his moustache, one that would rival Joseph Stalin's trademark 'stache, was a lesson in futility meets humility. Judd Moore never resuscitated the moustache again. Vanity has a way of winning either way sometimes. My Dad always told me that grooming your face is like having a big patch of land all your own.

"You can mow the grass or let it grow. It's your land and your decision. It shouldn't matter what other people think about how it looks."

I only saw two pictures of my Papaw with his moustache. He had a different look of confidence to him in those pictures. Thereafter – Papaw Judd never sought out the truth about what happened to his fine moustache. Figuring he had shaved half of it off while he was drunk or someone else had, he never questioned his loving wife and she never offered him the details of its loss. Roger, too, never *let the cat out of the bag.* Either way, it never truly mattered. Like the finger he had lopped off while chopping wood a few years before – it was merely a memory now – and buried somewhere in the halls and walls of a forgotten history.

My Dad grew out a fine moustache after completing his service in the United States Army. To my knowledge he has had one ever since. But he has never had a beard.

After shaving that blustery autumn morning in 1991 Judd patted his face dry with a towel, finished getting ready, and turned off the light. It was the 31st of November and there was much he planned to do this day. He had no idea this day would be his last

Suggested Listening: *Half a Man by George Jones* and Willie Nelson, *Wrinkles* by Diamond Rio

Education

If America believed in education, an average high school teacher would have a larger monthly income than any professional athlete or Hollywood actor makes in an entire year.

-JS Moore

Alcohol affects people differently. My father, for example, is much more talkative when he is drunk than when he is sober. His drunken ramblings and late night lectures were something I came to expect growing up. Sometimes the intensity of those meetings was difficult to sit through, but he - for the most part - meant only the best for whomever sat across from him. In a way I came to view him during our discussions as my shrink. No topic was taboo and no subject was off limits.

At age thirteen I remember him quite clearly making a fist and sticking out his pinky finger and telling Kevin and me, "This is your dick. You can play with it, piss with it, but always protect it." He paused strategically - to let the words sink in. My brother and I looked at each other. I smiled - kind of embarrassed. So did Kevin. Dad took a puff from his cigarette then rested the cancer stick on the side of the ashtray.

"Protect your dick," my father continued, "Think of it as a soldier marching into battle. Does your soldier wear a helmet?" Dad produced a small green party balloon from his shirt pocket and placed it over the tip of his pinky finger.

"Protection boys," he reminded very seriously, and then from that same shirt pocket he produced two small silver packages and tossed us each one. My first condom was kept in my wallet – where it formed a ring – and was never used.

We had long talks about everything from divorce and marriage, Vietnam, politics, evolution, how to make love to a woman, and goals. His other numerous lectures I will probably share in a later book.

But *The Reluctant Little Bird* story belongs here in *Understanding Apples*. It is a story my father acquired somewhere over the years and it should reverberate in the halls and walls of anyone's own heart.

Once upon a time, there was a little bird that refused to fly south for the winter. His friends and family tried to convince him that winter was coming and he should go, but the little bird was adamant.

"You'll freeze to death," one advised.

"Food will be scarce," another warned.

Finally, his loved ones gave up on convincing him and left on their long journey southbound, but the little bird remained behind. Pretty soon the weather turned bitter cold. The little bird began to shiver. A day went by and then we couldn't find a thing to eat. After a while, he decided he had made a mistake, so he too headed south. But he was too late and the weather descended upon him. As he flew, ice formed on his wings. He grew wearier with each strained flap of his little frozen wings until finally he fell to earth in a cow pasture, freezing and exhausted. He was convinced he was going to die. As he lay there, close to freezing to death, a cow came by and crapped on him. The manure warmed his body and wings. The bird realized he would live. He was so happy, he began to sing. A cat was passing by the little bird and heard the singing. The cat dug into the dung, uncovered the bird and promptly ate him.

There are three morals to this story:

1. Not everyone who craps on you is necessarily your enemy.
2. Not everyone who gets you out of the shit is necessarily your friend.
3. And, if you're warm and happy in a steaming pile of shit, keep your mouth shut.

Suggested Listening: *The Logical* Song by Supertramp

Bitter Harvest

We were born to die and we die to live. As seedlings of God, we barely blossom on earth; we fully flower in heaven.

- Russell M. Nelson

"Hoyt was my best friend," Dad managed with tears in his eyes. "I had the truck that day and had to pick Daddy up from work. Or I'd have been there with them."

Other Springdale boys were present when Hoyt got a cramp and drowned in Ft. Patrick Henry Lake (part of the Holston River). Jerry Taylor nearly drowned trying to save him.

"He was a strong swimmer," my Dad told the newspaper.

Opal had her teeth pulled and wasn't able to attend Hoyt's funeral. Judd didn't go. He wasn't the funeral service type.

So Roger was there at the burial service without his parents to help say good-bye to his very best friend. Hoyt's favorite song was Sugar Shack by Jimmy Gilmer and the Fireballs.

I picture Hoyt balancing on a railroad track and

singing this song with his arm stretched out at either side. And I am reminded that however brief a life is here on this tired Earth it should be made the best of. Hoyt drank in each day with a vigorous and passionate spirit. He loved life. Shouldn't we all?

There's a crazy little shack beyond the tracks
And ev'rybody calls it the sugar shack
Well, it's just a coffeehouse and it's made out of wood
Expresso coffee tastes mighty good
That's not the reason why I've got to get back
To that sugar shack, whoa baby
To that sugar shack. Yeh, yeh, yeh, our sugar shack

There is a small monument at Springdale Baptist with a Time Capsule that tells what was in the news in 1964 – the year Hoyt was taken from us. His memory survives, though. It always will. To this day my Dad has a framed 8X10 of Hoyt Bowen hung with loving pride upon the wall. I remember first asking him who was in that picture. I was just a little boy when I began hearing wonderful stories about his very best friend, Hoyt Bowen.

Suggested Listening: *Sugar Shack* by Jimmy Gilmer and the Fireballs

Busted Up

For believe me: the secret for harvesting from existence the greatest fruitfulness and greatest enjoyment is - to live dangerously.

- Friedrich Nietzsche

There was an old bootlegging joint on Main Street ran by Clint Barrett. Everyone that knew about it just called it Clint's Place. When Roger was home on leave from Vietnam he and his father Judd were sitting at the bar at Clint's Place having a cold one or three when suddenly a skirmish broke out between two big men, each well over 300 pounds. Fights were pretty common to the establishment and Clint usually let them go on as long as they weren't wrecking the place. One guy, however, had fallen back onto a card table and not only ruined his patrons' poker game, but had smashed in the table as well. When Roger went to rise from his stool to separate the men, his father casually tugged down on his arm and advised in a low voice,

"Pay them no mind. *Keep your shirt on.* This don't concern us."

The grizzled and permanently grumpy Clint Barrett

slammed the butt of a twelve-gauge shotgun onto the bar and shouted,

"Get the Friggin' hell outta here ya lard ass bastards!"

The two guys took their tussle elsewhere and no one followed them out the door for the outcome.

In the early Nineteen Seventies when Roger had returned from eighteen months of duty in South Korea, he and his father were sitting at Clint's Place in their usual spots when a small angry man walked over to Judd Moore and poured a beer over his head. Judd rose from his stool and with one hand already had the man lifted by his throat. He moved across the room with the man in tow and advised, "You're toting an ass-whoopin', shithead." Then he slammed the man against a wall and let him fall down into the floor, curled up into a heap and unconscious. Judd returned to his seat and didn't have an answer as to why the man might have wanted a row with him other than, "Roger, people sometimes just do some stupid shit. Someone probably dared the son-of-a-bitch to provoke me."

Suggested Listening: *I Love This Bar* by Toby Keith

Uprooted

Wicked people are always surprised to find ability in those that are good.

- Marquis De Vauvenargues

Like other virile males (and a handful of females) on Long Island – Judd Moore had earned quite a reputation fighting on weekends. Folks didn't usually fistfight because they had a score to settle, but because they just wanted to see who was toughest. Men from all parts of the area (Blair's Gap, Beech Creek, Bloomingdale, ← the Killer Bees) actually came to Long Island to mix it up and tangle with anyone they might have heard about word of mouth or word from "the Mouth of the South" Claude Russell. Claude is part alligator, all mouth and no ears. Claude knew the Stump Brothers needed extinguished, although they were friends of his, so he planted a tale about Judd Moore in their ear and knew what the end result would be. Claude is a talker and a fine teller of tales, a Highland area barber who wears no kilt.

On Main Street late one evening Judd Moore made his way toward the Old Gem to shoot a game or six of pool –

maybe hustle a game – or maybe just kid the waitress there he thought was pretty. As he passed Claude Russell and Fred Stump huddled close by the street he didn't expect Fred to approach him like he was up to no good. He didn't expect what came next

Claude's brother Ken, then a Main street barber/now a Lynn Garden businessman, witnessed Fred come through the front entrance of The Gem. Fred was ailing something awful and clutching his back, bent over like an old man left without a walker and trying to stand erect.

"What the hell happened to you," Ken asked.

"I made a mistake," Fred shared.

"Shit Fred – did you walk out in front of a dump truck or somethin'?"

"No – even worse. I retched up and slugged Judd Moore, blindsided him in the back of the head. That sum-bitch grabbed a hold of me and body-slammed me right there on Main Street."

"What's Galley say?"

"Ain't told him yet."

The door to the Gem swung open and Judd Moore stepped in slow, and then made his way calmly over to the bar where the pretty waitress was smiling at him.

"How 'bout a game," Ken asked him.

"Sure Ken, in a minute. Little Stump want to play, too?" Judd responded.

"Sure,"

"Is he worth a damn at *Cutthroat*?"

Ken bit his lip and looked over to his shaky grade school friend, Fred Stump, then managed with a laugh, "No – he ain't worth a taste of shit biscuit at Cutthroat, Judd. But his brother Galley is."

Ken Russell and Judd Moore had later fought around one another, but never with each other, each man testing who was toughest in the original Kingsport version of *Fight Club*, a prequel to Chuck Palahniak's fine novel. But I will stick to the first rule of the Kingsport chapter of *Fight Club* and not talk about it.

I am told by many that the Stump Brothers, Galley and Fred, wrecked havoc anywhere they went – be it Highland, West View, Long Island or any road they went down. Galley was of mammoth proportions – well over two hundred and fifty pounds and he was tall, too – around six foot two inches – as big as any professional wrestler was at the time. Galley was often thought to be drunk when he was sober because he was rowdy all the time, didn't say much, and when he did it was in a cynical mumble. Fred, the younger brother, was smaller – closer to two hundred pounds and he was a bit younger than his older brother. He was the brains of the outfit - if there was one. It was said the Stump Brothers were about *as useful as rubber lips on a woodpecker*. They were hot headed and bullied anyone they pleased. The Stumps actually sought out fights with folks with reputations of violence – to make a name for themselves - until one fiasco rendezvous when they crossed paths with the wrong man at *Ye Old Brown Jug*.

Judd Moore cooled the boys off, doused them with his left hand – the one made of iron - and a then a right hook – the one of steel. Galley got these first two blows with his face, and then Fred Stump took a forearm in the throat and was hurled across Dood Hunt's lap who helped Fred to his feet as Judd Moore grabbed the younger Stump and led him outside. Finishing out the ass whooping of the Stumps would be more difficult out on this side of town – *the Five Points* – where the riled up and ready cohorts of the Stumps waited for the results on curbside and joined in on the altercation soon enough. Judd Moore would have to outwit this crowd if he was to uproot the Stumps once and for all.

He was kicked, punched, and gouged by the Stumps and their posse of beatniks but he stayed on his feet and did something he hadn't done since he was a boy. He ran. He fled like some tormented mouse who was given an angry chase by the riff raff cats of the *Five Points*.

The Five Points - I want to mention in this case are not only a sharing of virtues but a sharing of vices – something plentiful in seedy parts of Kingsport at the time. It might have been that Judd Moore was to be wiped clean from this world right then and there. Had his pursuers had their way he might very well have ended up like so many other fine people of the day who, too, were just trying to get by during a difficult time.

Judd Moore was mad, but he was a survivor, and he was strong. He stopped up on Charlemont street and lifted a stop sign out from the ground, then he fought off the men – swatting away their knives and splitting open whatever skull got closest. He was left alone by those boys after that.

The problem was – even after Judd had settled down and didn't go looking for trouble – it still would manage to find him.

"I was born naked like the rest of these guys," he said, "and if it don't beat all I ever seen – I was put here to make a dent, to raise a little hell, stir up the fire some. I want people to know I was here. It don't make no difference if I was the damn president of the United States of America or some bean farmer. I've started off with empty pockets, but worked every day the good Lord has given me and I've not complained. But folks are gonna know I was here."

A man can only hope when he passes on that he is remembered. My Papaw developed a reputation that folks still talk about today.

Suggested Listening: *The Fightin' Side of Me* by Merle Haggard

SLIVER

Spare minutes are the Gold-dust of time; the portions of life most fruitful in good and evil; the gaps through which temptations enter.

- Anonymous

The recliner in which he always sat was covered in a very worn and tattered lime green fabric. A round gray vinyl ottoman about one foot high and one and a half feet around served as a table for his plate of apple slices. He would lightly salt each one of the slices then turn on the television to watch a boxing match, a Western film, or one of his favorite shows. He enjoyed *The Dukes of Hazzard, Gunsmoke, Bonanza, Rawhide,* and

The Rifleman. Late at night, he watched the local news, then *Benny Hill* before he went to bed. He watched the television with utter seriousness and disliked any noise that was not coming from the nineteen-inch black and white Zenith in front of him. Bringing a sliver to his lips, he would take a bite, savoring the flavor of that Red Delicious apple – still watching intently. During commercials, he was telling quick stories about his life to us grandkids. His stories were about drunken nights playing cards or billiards, brawling, and growing up during hard times.

"One time," he explained, "I woke up to the sound of thunder – like the voice of God grumblin' down at me with a quick crack and a rolling boom - with the pouring rain nearly drowning me in a sewer ditch just outside an old bootlegging joint on Long Island. I tried to stand but found the sting of my wounds keeping me down. I'd been jumped by a swarm of heathens – proud sons o' bitches who'd heard tale of me whoopin' a relative of theirs."

"Months earlier I'd tossed that sorry sack around the horse stables for swindling me at Five-card Stud. Sure, I hated to lose, but losing to a smooth cheat with quick hands and wits was a whole other story. There'd been fools killed for lesser things," he looked down at the plate - but somehow through it - with an empty stare as if in a trance for a moment, then continued, "not by me, of course. However, I'd roughed him up good, sliced him with my knife, walloped him in the mouth with a tobacco stick, and knocked out some of his teeth. I stepped on one of his hands with my foot then held his head against a fresh pile of manure and told him I'd better never see his sorry ass around again. I took the money and divided it amongst the other players. I'd forgotten about it until the night the ruffians ambushed me."

"As I stepped from my truck I heard one of 'em

whisperin', 'That's him. That's Judd Moore.' I knew something weren't right. I wasn't liquored up just yet, and if I had been, I think I'd stood a better chance. A seasoned lookin' country boy wearin' bib overalls rounded the far corner and positioned himself by the entrance of the buildin' with his arms folded and a pitchfork within arms reach. He had a mean sway about him and an evil eye. If there'd been horns on his head and he had a pointy tail I think I'd been ready to send him back to a blazin' hell, but he was still young – a little older than Roger was at the time – maybe nineteen or twenty. He was homegrown. He was thick with broad shoulders and weighed plenty more than me. His beer-gut stuck out like a pregnant gal ready to burst. He was already pretty drunk and I could tell he was ready to pick a fight.

'You Judd Moore?' he spoke up.

I stopped my advance and looked about me. Two more home-growns moved around behind me ten or so feet away while another knelt watchin' intently near an old pick-up. I didn't know these lads, but it was apparent they knew me.

'Who wants to know?' I asked.

'You roughed up my Pa. He can't chew his food right or use his right hand so well. I aim to whip you good,' the homegrown by the truck hollered out. He, too, had been drinking. He was a tad smaller than the other three, but still bigger than me. Though I wasn't exactly sure who they were talking about, I had a good idea so I said back, 'He had it comin', kid.' The two behind me rushed forward and I stepped off to the side to let them pass, kicking one of them behind the knee and sending him face first into the gravel. 'Home-grown' with the weapon waited his turn. I was thinking this whole time I didn't want to hurt these boys, but I didn't want to get hurt either. 'Face First' got up cussing me and calling me everything you could think up. I'd heard it all before. The loud one from the truck joined the other three to my front and it was quite a feelin' I had deep down that someone was about to get a lickin'. But, I didn't expect another one to come from behind. Facing the four home-growns, I got hit upside the head by a two by four, I believe. Hell, maybe it was a tobacco stick. I remember lookin' up at the four boys as they were kickin' me, then noticing the final dealer was the swindler himself, Dew Bowles."

I interrupted his story, "Doo. His name was Doo – as in doo-doo?"

My Papaw chuckled, "He was a piece alright," then shaking his head from side to side his face got very solemn as he continued, "I remember him liftin' that pitchfork up and stabbin' it down on my chest. A surge of pain and shock struck into me like a lightnin' bolt splittin' a tree trunk. And I must have passed out because that is all I remember of the beaten. Had I been liquored up real good I'd not have remembered a thing 'bout it."

"We're you hurt really bad Papaw?" I asked him concerned.

He sat sedated in memory, staring down again as if he remembered plainly, then all at once glared me in the eyes and with a grimness I'd never seen from him and he answered, "Oh yeah. I'd never been beat down like that. Never. But it was as if I was supposed to remember it – else I'd been wasted with alcohol and just drowned in that ditch-line like a poor drunken fool."

"Did you get them back?"

"Nope. Didn't have to. Some weeks later Dew Bowles and his son Dewey were both killed while trying to steal another man's cows. The boy was shot through the heart by a farmer I know and Ole' Dew was trampled to death by a group of spooked livestock that didn't take kindly to the sound of gunshot. Cattle rustling was a dangerous business to be in back then. I'd felt sorry for their families, but not for them. They were both a different breed of person than what I'd finagled with in the bootleggin' joints, pool halls, and hole in the road rough spots. They were the kinda folk it's best to steer clear from in life."

"How do you know someone is like that?" I asked him.

He bit into another piece of apple and handed me another slice. I held it and looked at it as I waited for his answer. He chewed his up slow and swallowed it, then said, "Well Jason, it's like this: Sometimes you just know in your gut somebody can't be trusted. Other times it's hard to say. Hmmm. Always keep a wolf to your front and never let him behind you or he'll bite you. There's the loner wolf and there's also those who hunt in a pack. You might see one wolf, but there can always be more. You understand?"

"I think so."

The commercial break was over and *Gunsmoke* commenced. Matt Dillon had his hands full with some no good heathens himself. He was punching and scraping and being knocked around some but ended up on top. My Papaw watched the scuffle from the edge of his chair and seemed to help Sheriff Dillon along with a jab and a right hook. I sat there eating the apple, but digesting the old man's story.

For a good while I thought about just how bad it would be to get jumped by five ruffians. My Papaw had been whipped almost fatally. I had never been cut or stabbed at that time in my life, much less by a pitchfork, but hearing about Papaw Judd getting gigged like a frog makes me cringe to this very day. He suffered a punctured neck – only a centimeter from his jugular vein. The other prong went all the way through his right forearm and into his right side just below the ribcage. He leaned forward in the ditch with the tool still sticking through him and somehow managed to get to his feet. Grabbing the handle with his left hand, he pulled it away from him but the pain was too severe to continue. He took a deep breath then let it out. Lightning flashed the night sky to life as Judd Moore removed the pitchfork from his body and whispered a scream of agony. He somehow managed to drive himself to the clinic. To hear my Papaw tell the story it was as if it was just another day to him

"I've still got that goddamn fork in the tool shed," he kidded me.

My Dad informed me that Papaw's demeanor changed greatly after the assault because of a brief conversation they had with one another.

"I'd better quit this shit, Roger," he stated, "or I might end up killin' someone."

"Well Daddy," Roger advised, "this isn't your first bout with the reaper. You might get killed yourself."

This simple statement was a revelation to my Papaw Judd, striking a nerve in the man who'd lived his whole life feeling invincible. Soon after their talk, my Papaw stopped drinking for good.

Suggested listening: *The Wild Side of Life* by Hank Thompson

Stitches

Up until he had open heart surgery Judd Moore didn't do much traveling. I am told he was only available in three states; working, drunk, or unconscious, but either way he was unavailable.

- JS Moore

J udd Moore had two belly buttons... not really. The top button was actually a deep scar from a knife wound inflicted to him in an alleyway off Main Street in the early 1950's. He walked with his boots filled with blood all the way to the clinic on Brook Circle where Dr. McConnell advised him that if it hadn't been for his stomach muscles that the puncture would have been a fatal one.

Guy McKinney used to tell my Papaw to "get in church – do something with your life – let God in. Stop with the drinkin' and get right."

To which my Papaw responded, "You are no better than me. I drink and you smoke."

Mr. McKinney threw his one pack of cigarettes away and never smoked again.

My Papaw became the man my Mamaw thought he should be after he had open-heart surgery in the early

1980's. He began to go to church soon after. For her – this was all that mattered. The good Lord would do the rest. Like every one of us, Judd Moore was a sinner – and a notorious one at that. My Papaw didn't know too much going into Springdale Baptist church for only the third time in his life. The first time he was in the church was after he helped lay the foundations for the building, borrowing a bulldozer from Tennessee Eastman and driving it across the Sluice. That was in 1946 and this was the first time he spent any time around the preacher L.C. Collins. Pastor Collins showed Judd around the newly built structure – one a then twenty-eight year old Judd helped to complete.

"These doors are always open," the Pastor reminded him.

The second time he was in Springdale Baptist Church he wasted with moonshine, *as drunk as a skunk*, and he demanded his wife come home to make him breakfast after a night of mischief at *Five Points*. Opal left after his insistence went to vulgarities – to save the congregation more of a scene.

But the third time he entered the church was after his surgery to inform those in attendance that he was a changed man and that an angel had appeared by his hospital bed giving him a choice: he could go on to a fiery hell or he could mend his ways. When my grandfather was fighting for his life after the surgery, little did he know that a good friend of his – Pastor L.C. Collins – had passed away just a few rooms down the hallway. I believe Pastor Collins made one final visit to Judd Moore and that visit won my Papaw to the Lord.

Suggested Listening – My Own Kind of Hat by Merle Haggard, My Buckets Got a Hole In It, I Saw The Light by Hank Williams,

Fresh

The difference between a moral man and a man of honor is that the latter regrets a discreditable act, even when it has worked and he has not been caught.

- H.L. Mencken

After the murder of Carl Thomas "Zeke" Cleek his friends and family thought enough of their fallen relative to always keep fresh flowers upon his grave at Holston View Cemetery in Weber City, VA. The trouble was, though, each time new flowers were brought to his graveside the old ones had disappeared. After this had occurred several times Buck Click devised a plan to catch the culprit. He stationed Peter "Peezer" Halkleroad at the cemetery. Peezer, who was known to stutter and couldn't talk plain, was actually quite the ladies man back then. And he was garrisoned up in the cemetery one evening fooling around with this girl when a car drove up slow, with its headlights turned off, then stopped and a frumpy man stepped out. He walked straight over to Zeke Cleek's grave and removed the flowers. It was the florist. Before long Peezer gathered up his clothes and reported the news to Buck. The

Cleeks sought justice and the florist was taken before the judge who was ashamed,

"You know this kind of scandalous garbage shouldn't be happening... not in this fine city. I could put you away for a while, ruin your business for this kind of behavior, but I won't. Your sentence, sir, is one you'll be faced with very often and that is maintaining fresh flowers on this man's grave – at no cost to his family."

The florist soon after developed an allergy to plants and he sold his shop, but the new proprietors kept the flower shop name, thus binding them to the sentence. To this day, I am told, some fifty years later, there are still fresh flowers kept upon Zeke Cleek's grave.

One bad apple doesn't have to spoil the bunch. It just serves to show that apples can go bad.

Suggested Listening: *The Garden* by Vern Gosdin

EDEN

Rather your dauntless virtue, whom the pain
Of death denounced, whatever thing Death be,
Deterred not from achieving what might lead
To happier life, knowledge of Good and Evil?
Of good, how just! Of evil-if what is evil
Be real, why not known, since easier shunned?

- John Milton

"When he came home, it was late," Dad told me, "he had on work boots, blue jeans and a white nylon jacket covered in blood. Dad didn't own a white nylon jacket and it wasn't his blood."

In October of 1960 Judd Moore had just finished showering in the Big Shop, Number 156, when the silence was deafened by an explosion, the ground shook and windows of every building within two miles were blown out. Judd's eardrums pounded and then buzzed continuous like some alarm going off in his brain. He had his blue jeans and boots on and rushed outside with his shirt off. Hot metal rained from the sky and the air was filled with dark smoke and it made his lungs burn like they'd been placed in an oven. He retrieved a handkerchief to cover his mouth and he surveyed the damage.

Tennessee Eastman Company was like a war torn battlefield and the places he knew were gone now. There were smaller - lesser explosions like the plant was under attack. People were crying, some running for their life, some trying to help whoever needed assistance. Sirens roared like a thousand wolves moaning - howling into the chaos; the shattered void. Order was left asunder and Judd knew he should flee, but he didn't. His chiseled muscular image was seen running to wherever he could help out and the hot metal was still falling with the ash and soot but the little burns failed to deter the man. He could barely breathe because the fire in his lungs. Coughing now - his eyes were a campfire - a blaze.

Two men, their flesh burned badly, ran naked past Judd, screaming and running from the steel drums. One man's eyebrows were singed clean off.

"Here buddy," a man in uniform yelled to him, tossing Judd a white nylon jacket. Without thinking he slipped on the jacket, then he heard a man moaning over all the noise and he sought him out - followed his cries onto the stairwell of a place he'd helped to build a decade before. And then Judd ascended the metal steps and called out, "Keep talkin' to me. I am on my way, friend!"

Dad said he carried one feller out alive that had his leg torn clean off. That is the only time Roger Moore saw his father cry when he Judd Moore was sober. Judd came out of his truck like a shot and ran to his wife Opal and hugged her tighter than a bear and he wept and he shook and she was strong for him. The children knew she loved him. She always did. Debbie and Roger hugged them both and they all cried together - glad he was safe. Opal began to pray for the families of all those victims and Judd Moore wept. Dad grieved just speaking about the explosion only briefly. He was fourteen when it happened.

Too often someone is dubbed a hero because they scored thirty-two points in a championship final and drained a three-pointer as the buzzer sounded to win the game. Too often someone is called a living legend because they've been singing songs for twenty years. But legendary status and a title of hero shouldn't be *passed out like candy* to children. Those decorations should be reserved for the brave few who have the gumption to really make a difference when an emergency situation takes place. Those few whose egos and wallets aren't inflated – who boldly run into a deadly situation for their neighbor to help the very best they can or know how to, and humbly walk away from the situation without expecting credit to be given. Those are the real heroes. It just goes to show us that heroism comes in many forms in this day and age. There were heroes on September 11th of 2001. As the world remembers that day of infamy and despair – the residence of this region who witnessed the explosion at Eastman in 1960 all remember where they were and what they were doing. Some "higher ups" were taking action in questionable ways like determining the best excuse as to why it happened. Why did so many have to lose their life for this "accident"? Many were praying, huddled together on street corners or within the walls of their churches or homes. And there were a few unrecognized heroes in October of 1960 who asked for no credit, too.

Accidents are often mishaps that could have easily been prevented. Those of us who know the truth are silent. But the truth – the truth – *the Truth* – is all that is important in this life.

Suggested Listening: *Help Somebody* by Van Zant

Worm Holes

To see the world in a grain of sand, and to see heaven in a wild flower, hold infinity in the palm of your hands, and eternity in an hour.

- William Blake

That November morning of 1991 found Judd Moore busy with his morning rituals: McDonalds for breakfast and some sitting down with his friends shooting the bull with their b.b. gun tongues and nudging the beast into the barn for castration. A few short months earlier the new McDonalds had finally opened up. The new building lay within reach of the old building, but the old building was perfectly fine. It was the Powers That Be who insisted on the buildings location adjustment of around thirty feet so that a small road could feed in on both sides of Mac's Crack and Long John's. Progress!

"Why the hell they gonna tear down the other one," Papaw went on, *"Why can't they use the old one as a shelter or something for the homeless?"*

"Cause this old world is run by 'the Man'," Jimmy answered him with confidence.

"Well, I'd like to meet 'the Man' and wallop him right good with a ball-peen hammer," Preacher added with undying conviction.

"It's a crock of horse shit is what it is," Judd told them.

As I lay awake with my mind swirling with questions unanswered inside - the dark room is silent with blackness engulfing, then suddenly my eyes open wide to a creature unseen from the depths of my dream and the very abyss of self-doubt. At first I'm afraid

Then the feeling evades and my arms in an instant reach out. My fingers touch nothing like a mime in routine, but something still lingers below; an apparition is circling, slowly just swirling beneath me a spirit aglow.

I'd like to travel back in time, ask Judd Moore one question that came flooding through my mind like the words that might never come – like a song unwritten with lyrics unshared but melody hummed.

After the Eastman Bridge collapsed in the late 1960's it was never repaired. There was apparently a good reason not to fix the bridge and the city of Kingsport and Tennessee Eastman Company resolved to cast a blind eye on the thoroughfare's demise. The Long Island community began to be acquired little by little as the Tennessee Eastman Company expanded. In the late 1980's and early 1990's Eastman's desire for the properties increased and soon their methods became downright aggressive. All but a handful of families had sold their homes and some of the long-term businesses had began to dissolve also – due to alcohol being made legal by the state of Tennessee in the late 70's. I've heard most families were compensated well to relocate, while others were completely shafted with low offers, shady bank schemes, and corporate politicking.

Some fine homes were being destroyed, leveled, and soon invisible all together in the name of progress. But one stretch that had been abandoned stood out like a South Dakota ghost town in the shadows of Industry. It was here that my Papaw would meet his destiny, here that he would receive his calling, here that he would unexpectedly bid us farewell at the former house of Bill Carr behind Doc Stout's Store.

Late November of 1991, my senior year of high school, my Papaw Judd was removing wire from a wall in an old run down house that used to be Bill Carr's (Stick Man from the story **Pecking Order**) home on Long Island. He always stripped wire of the covering and saved the copper - to later take to the recycle place. It was raining heavily as he worked. No one knew what he was doing that day really. Everyone knew he'd gone to McDonalds for breakfast but didn't know where he'd gone afterwards - just that he was to pick up my Mamaw around noon to take her to her hair appointment at Penney's where my cousin Tammy worked as a beautician. Well, he never showed to pick her up. Like I said earlier, Judd was a punctual person. Time ran on and soon she became worried so she called my Dad - who drove over to her house from work immediately. By the time I was getting home from school it was around 5pm or so. The day was just like any other, except for all the rain. There was a note on the counter that read, "Come to your Grandparents' house." When I got there a police cruiser was parked outside. And my Dad and his sister Debbie's car were in the driveway. The officers had just finished asking their questions and getting a description of Papaw's truck and a photo of him as well. After they left I got to talk to Barbara, my stepmother, who explained to me that Papaw was missing and that he never came home to pick my

Mamaw up, etc. They thought maybe he'd picked up a hitchhiker and was made to drive them somewhere, or that he had somehow gotten hurt and was nowhere near people or a phone. The police were looking for his truck. And my Dad and I went driving around different places we'd thought he might be. We had no luck in finding him. My Papaw's friends were called and still no one had a clue where he was. The next day around 1pm I was called at school and told to go to my Mamaw's when I got out - that Papaw had been found. I was excited to hear he'd been found and hurried to Mamaw's house. When I got there I ran onto the porch and Barbara greeted me with a hug.

"Where was he?" I asked her.

"Have a seat," she told me. We sat down and she broke the news to me that Papaw was inside a house pulling wiring from the walls sometime the day before and the roof collapsed - killing him instantly. I would later find out that my Papaw's good friends, the Boss Man Clay Rodefer and the Stick Man Bill Carr, found him, crowbar in hand, hanging half out in the rain and the other half buried beneath the roof as if he'd ran when he heard it falling but still didn't make it out. He'd been rained on. His truck was parked beside the road, unlocked. There was still several hundred dollars in an envelope in the dash and a few personal checks to be deposited also where Papaw had been paid for doing odd jobs for people. He was 73, my best friend, and it came as a complete and utter shock to me that he was gone.

The autopsy report came to say several things about my Papaw, that his heart was unusually hard. His neck and ribs were shattered. He died, though, piddling - working, staying busy. He was quite an example of human life. He was the best kind of man to those who loved him. And he was the worst to those who disliked him.

I've never seen so many people at a funeral. Some people came to pay their respects, while many couldn't believe he was dead, others came just to be sure.

Before his death I had enlisted in the United States Army as a military police officer, but the truth is - telling stories was the only thing I felt like I was good at - joining the military was merely to make my Dad proud and show him I could set a goal and accomplish it.

I mostly wrote poetry then. I wrote one poem especially for my Papaw Judd for Father's Day of 1991. It was titled "*The Lonely One*". I read it to him and gave him a typed copy. He kept that poem folded up and tucked away in his front shirt pocket. Sometimes he'd ask me to read it aloud to him again. He seemed to enjoy the poem. From time to time he would show it to his friends at Mac's Crack, too. It made me feel good. That poem means much more to me now than it did when I gave it to him. It was as if he was giving it back to me - what it meant to him. It was folded in his shirt pocket the day he was killed on Long Island.

The Lonely One

For a while I watch the morning sun
Rise above the hill.
And for a moment I feel I'm the lonely one
With time just standing still
But when I stood alone last night
Beneath the stormy sky
I thought I heard a raven take flight
And it moved my spirit high.
So I wondered: where are the dreamers?
Are they lost planting their precious trees?

Trees of time that at no cost
Control our destinies.
A single leaf on the deadest of trees
Is fighting a furious wind
The tree may fall
To answer Life's call
But the leaf might slowly descend.

To my knowledge – Judd Moore was the last man killed on Long Island. If the Cherokee curse that "No white man would ever find peace on Long Island" were true – I believe my Papaw's death negated that spell... one that lasted more than two hundred years.

I do believe he found peace.

Suggested Listening: *Landslide* by The Dixie Chicks

An Invitation to the Reader

Although I chose early on to avoid the complexities and dissection in evaluating the history, myth, and origins of the apple - I do still feel the apple deserves much more of a tribute and homage than the few pages of this book. I will write more on Judd Moore, his influences, relations, and adventures. *The Orange Blossom Special* and an addition to *Reservoir Dog*, among many other stories (written and unwritten), will be a part of the next compilation.

Again, there are still more stories I have written and will be writing about Judd Moore, Buzz McClain, Hack Cleek and some of the other characters within these pages. Entire books could be written on any of these individuals. But I leave this open-ended with a unique invitation: I believe in the power of stories and welcome anyone in the Tri-Cities Region with a story to tell to put those stories to paper or contact me and I will do it for you and possibly include it in this next body of work. I can be reached by mail at:

Understanding Apples

c/o JS Moore
2306 Abbott Drive
Johnson City, TN 37601

Please include SASE for prompt response. Don't let your history be forgotten! Remember:
Nothing has really happened until it has been recorded.

-- Virginia Woolf

JSmoor6@charter.net

(423)202-1371

Thank-you!

I would like to thank Joanne Uppendahl for her continued guidance, encouragement, and editing advice. A special thanks to the McClain, Rodefer, Bowen, Collins, and Cleek families. I would like to applaud my friends and family as well for their undying support of this book. There are too many folks to list. Thanks.

-JS Moore

UNDERSTANDING APPLES

Printed in the United States
79743LV00001B/34-51